Tales in the Waitākere Ranges

Auckland Writers

Auckland Writers

ISBN (Paperback) 978-1-0671490-93
ISBN (ebook) 978-1-0670828-5-7
Cover photography: Susan Glamuzina
Cover design and interior formatting: Melissa Gunn

Contents

Youth Section

End of Youth Section

Foreword

I can't believe we've managed to make four anthologies now! Five years ago, I was sitting in the Wintergardens when I had the idea of collecting stories from different writers, set in the Auckland Domain. We've now published Tales' anthologies about the Auckland Domain, Dominion Road, the Hauraki Gulf and the Waitākere Ranges.

My first night living in Auckland was in the Waitākere Ranges. I organised a flat from a newspaper ad and moved in without previously meeting my flatmate. It turned out that I was so scared of him that I packed everything and moved out in the middle of that first night to stay in my car instead. I have either lived in the Waitākere Ranges, or at their feet ever since.

Being beach obsessed, I've spent so much time at Auckland's west coast beaches. There is something about black sand and wild waves that's therapeutic. When my children were young, they went to Arataki at least weekly. It was a chance to escape Auckland's concrete jungle and get amongst New Zealand nature at its best.

We took train trips to the water reserve, used metal detectors to look for shrapnel at Te Henga Bethells Beach, tented at Piha, and waited for the tide to go out before going into the cave at Maukatia Māori Bay.

My first ever poem was written for the inaugural Tales anthology, and the first poetry workshop I attended was at Piha with Anne Kennedy. We were challenged to write a poem about how the beach made us feel and then with large sticks we etched our poems into the sand. It was life changing. While preparing for this anthology, I taught a poetry workshop at Arataki and hope to have inspired others as Anne Kennedy has inspired me.

I'm so excited to share not just my journey but other people's experiences of this vibrant taonga, the phenomenal Waitākere Ranges.

Susan Glamuzina

It has been a blessing to get to know Bruce Wyness over the last few anthologies; he sadly passed away before this one could be launched. He was such a positive contributor who was so supportive with his constant kind words. Bruce touched the lives of many writers including those he has shared these anthologies with and he will be missed. We send our love to his family.

Starting a New Life

Bruce Wyness

Prologue

There is a 60-kilometre-long ecological corridor that runs from the Hauraki Gulf to the Waitākere Ranges. Known as the North-West Wildlink, it aims to create 'safe, connected and healthy habitats for native wildlife across Auckland' (Forest & Bird). These act as stepping stones between conservation hotspots such as the Hauraki Gulf Islands and the Waitākere Ranges.

Manu woke. He stayed motionless listening to the morning chorus. The whistle and clicks of Tūī, the *zip, pip* of Riflemen and the chattering of Saddlebacks. The sun was rising over the bush on Tiritiri Matangi Island. Morning dew deflected the rays across the leaves of the trees and bushes. The air was fresh and clear. Kiwi, Ruru and the little blue penguins had returned to their burrows and tree hollows, leaving the land to the daylight guardians.

Manu ruffled his wings, stretching and rising from his branch, his crimson belly and orange underwings on display. He called across the bush *kra-aa, kra-aa*. The call echoed around the valley and was returned by other Kākā. There were only a small number of native parrots on the island and their distinctive calls were clear in the morning air. Unlike most Kākā, Manu was an explorer, aloof and territorial and did not generally socialise with the other parrots. He and his partner, Rewa, were content to be a pair rather than part of the flock.

A thrumming echoed across the water but caused no concern to Manu. He had heard this sound many times over the summer months. It was the vessel carrying conservation staff, guides and visitors to the island. The topsides were painted cream with a blue stripe along the chine. It rode easily on the ocean swell.

With winter approaching, fruit and flowers were becoming scarce. Manu knew that the feed stations would need to be replenished with sugar water. Tūī, Hihi and Bellbirds would line the branches along the tracks to drink the sweet liquid. The cicada chorus had gone, and Manu was already eating autumn fare of leaves from kōwhai and lucerne. It was clear to him that there were too many birds competing for the same food.

In the distance across the water, on a clear day, he could see large tree covered hills on the horizon. He didn't know these were the Waitākere Ranges.

He sensed there would be food there. For some time, he had mused on flying to see. He and Rewa were still breeding each season, and they needed to have a good supply of native fruits to ensure they could continue. Manu shuffled along the branch bowing, bouncing and pushing Rewa with his foot and beak. His *tsee-tsee-tsee* call showing his intent. He shuffled away, watching for a reaction from her. Rewa did not move, she showed no interest in him. He would try again another day.

There was still time to mate and raise a new chick this season. Rewa had proven to be a good mother. They were a team and worked well together, Manu foraging for food to feed Rewa and the babies.

Manu scanned the bush around him, his eyes keen and unblinking, observing the other birds. This island was a safe place, but they wanted better. Together they had decided to leave Tiritiri Matangi and fly towards the Waitākere Ranges seeking a place to start a new life.

They would first fly across the water to Whangaparāoa. It would be the first step of their adventure. Manu could assess what food was available and find a safe spot to rest for the night. The decision made, they left the branch of the Puriri tree and flew towards the west, where the sun set at the end of each day.

Manu and Rewa circled awhile looking for a suitable tree to land on. They dived down into the bush, weaving between the trees, seeking a resting place. Rewa chose a Pōhutukawa tree with a deep hollow where a branch met the trunk, a perfect spot to rest for the night. It extended over the Weiti River near a large tract of bush. There were berries and nectar close by and the thick canopy gave them shelter.

In the evening light they saw possums in the trees around them. Manu was wary and watched them carefully positioning himself above the hollow branch Rewa was sleeping in.

The sound of Rewa screeching *kraak, kraak* startled Manu. He turned, a stoat was on the branch below him, hissing and baring its teeth. He leapt down with his claws extended and bit the stoat on the neck, drawing blood.

He bit again tearing the skin and raked his claws over the stoat's back. With a howl the stoat leapt away trying to dislodge Manu. He let it go and swooped back to check on Rewa. She was unharmed.

Kra-aa, kra-aa echoed through the bush as Manu sent his cry out the next morning. They ate berries and insects from the surrounding trees before setting off towards the Waitākere Ranges. Staying close to the treetops they flew on over the land heading west for an hour then stopped in a large, wooded area near the upper reaches of the Waitematā. Manu felt this was not a good place to stay so after feasting on seeds and nectar they flew on.

Below them was a ribbon of green. Trees and bush running across the land in a continuous strip connecting large swaths of bush sanctuaries. On either side there were open fields and buildings, farm land with herds of cows and sheep. Instinctively Manu knew these places could expose them to danger so he avoided flying over them, sticking to the eco-corridor that provided food and safety for their journey. The horizon was clearer now and he could see vast expanses of trees and bush. In the distance he saw the deep blue of an ocean and the black sands that separated the two. They decided to rest another night so that they could arrive the following day with plenty of time to explore.

Their second night was under the canopy of a large Kauri [tree] close to the eco-corridor. Manu stripped the bark off some branches with his large beak searching for grubs and sap. He and Rewa preened themselves in a water filled tree bowl 10 metres above the forest floor and fussed with their feathers. These flights were longer than what they had been used to but not too arduous as they were big and strong. As the sun set, they selected a limb near the top of the Kauri to settle in and begin their sleep cycle. A serious of short naps separated by tiny awake moments, this sequence continued throughout the night.

The moonlight seeped through the tree cover and scattered beams across the forest floor. A Kiwi padded silently through the undergrowth, tapping its beak on the ground, sniffing and probing for food. A pair of rats scurried among the forest debris, collecting material for their nests.

Morning dawned warm and bright with a clear sky. Manu and Rewa stretched their wings, pushed off from the Kauri and flew for a while, weaving through the trees, seeking a water source. They found a small stream, dipped their beaks in, tilted their heads back and swallowed. Now, they were ready. They flew west.

The Waitākere rainforest opened up in front of them. It was huge and extended along the coast in both directions. They flew towards the black sand then along the shoreline and back. People were riding the waves on boards and bathing on the beach. The sights and sounds of waves crashing on the shore, voices loud and harsh, seagulls rising and falling with the surf flow, piles of driftwood contrasted with the unbroken expanse of the forest. Giant Kauri and Tawa trees rose above the canopy adding to the splendour. Together they flew along the coast just above the treetops. Instinctively they knew this would be their new home.

Manu and Rewa swooped under the canopy and into the forest. They explored and inspected the native trees. Some towering giants, some smaller, some not seen before. Many had berries or seeds and there were numerous streams and pools. Together they searched over a large area before settling on a mature Tawa. Overlooking a waterfall and with a hollow between the trunk and a branch 15 metres above the ground, it was a perfect place to build a nest. Manu used his beak to enlarge the entrance, pulling the soft wood away and dropping it into the base of the hollow.

They rested side by side. Manu shuffled closer and pushed Rewa with his beak and feet.

"*Tsee-tsee-tsee,*" he called. Rewa nudged him back.

"*Tsee-tsee-tsee,*" she replied. This was where they would raise their young.

Maybe living with a hoon of Kākā would be interesting. Being part of a gregarious flock could become part of their new life.

This was their home now.

Waitākere Fibre Art

Caroline Carlyle

Māori Tohutō of Love & Hope

Chris Reed

My grandmother was taught
 by a father from Tairāwhiti coast
the best way to repel the ravaging west
was to speak only in te reo Māori

me rangimārie she would add
 finishing any question off with an imperative
meaning 'be at peace' and 'take comfort'
You had to *take your time*, even if it meant simply filling your belly with air

When the language war came to Aotearoa it took away that comfort,
 a generational fight for linguistic sovereignty
she was twelve when she stopped.
a karanga fading in memory -

But when her first born came into the world
  a boy, like his mother, screaming from the nave her tongue
produced no other sound but
the one she knew by heart

again &   again &   again &
ano me   ano me   ano me
hoarsing her voice to a whimper
her own personal grenade before her pain, before her husband

in secret she stole the boy from the world
  collecting the occasional toheroa from Karekare beach
speaking bits she held captive in memory
letting the waves carry them back to land

but tides are strong

when I appeared she barely spoke
  no karakia or koha
another battle ground slipped
edged out to place names and greetings

tauria means attack, or assault
  because the war never left her
but lived in her gut
and it emptied her life

perhaps its best suited because

  tau also means to sing

under her breath when my father was not around just

loud enough for me to hear

just loud enough for me to learn

just loud enough for me to sing along

Encounter with Tīrairaka on the Upper Kauri Track

Lincoln Jaques

Little tīrairaka, a full universe
dwells within a single feather.
You found me as a shadow
cast from an old mātai. You were perched
on a knot sealed over a hundred
years, a wound that never closed.

You looked at me, a shadow starched
in the afternoon sun, frozen like a fly
glued in kauri gum. An unmoving eye—
sceptical. This is my life, you said, divided
into tantric parts.

The ancient canopy suffocates us
shaft of blue and grey fall between darkness
I pause on the track, breathe in the damp bark
the distant sound of the ocean echoes
through the trees where empty souls now walk.

And tīrairaka, you never finished telling me
everything you knew about the forest.
For I needed to take my leave
and with me my shadow
as you turned your head away.

Nothing permanent can remain in this place.

Melissa Gunn: Tīrairaka or pīwakawaka

Whoosh

Angela Campbell

Whoosh!
Is God simply slipstream from the wing of a tūī,
the divinity of air
around something songful that moves?

In his dark garb and ivory cravat,
he sits like a judge (the tūī, not God) warbling
"O is all of 'loneliness' moon-like and milk-like and deep."

He sings from the treetops
to some Creator or Destroyer
while bone flutes below
breathe mischief into the mist.

The canticle finds human ears.
Adam, first tramper of the day,
listens as he brushes his shoes.

Whoosh.

The Eel at Kitekite

Barbara Peterson

The eel that peeks
His face through the water
Shimmering like oil
Eyes hypnotic, fascinated
I never feel so seen
So valuable, as he stares
Intently, regarding my face
As if it were the shiniest prize
As if I were the holiest fish
Or an angel, he looks
At me and, what does he see
What does he see in me
That I can't see?

Barbara Peterson: Eel peeking

It Was a Huia

Sue Carpenter

No device Sunday! We got in the car and drove to the Waitākere Ranges. We walked on the five-minute track but it wasn't five minutes, more like 15 minutes downhill. It was meant to be a loop, but the track ended, and we had to climb back up the steep walkway. My brother, always energetic, ran first. At the top he tore off right instead of back to the car park, so we all had to trudge off after him.

Swoosh, a kererū dove over me. He was epic and if I had my phone, I would've snapped the best photo. Stupid device free day!

A chirp to my left, I watched a fantail chasing a moth through the ferns, darting around more than my brother. I ended up ages behind my family. The next bird that caught my eye had a long-curved beak. At first, I thought it was a tūī but instead of white tufts it had bright yellow on its face. I was sure I'd seen pictures of a bird like that at school. I wanted to take a photo – so frustrating. I wished I could call Mum and Dad back,to see, but I knew they would scare the bird off, so I watched her until she flew away over the Waitākere canopy.

That night when I got home, I sat down at my desk and sketched the bird. Dad came in and smiled said, 'Wow, I love your huia.'

'Is that what she was? I saw this bird on the walk today,' I told him.

'No way you did,' he said, 'the huia has been extinct for years.'

'I swear I saw this bird,' I told him.

Dad didn't believe me. The teachers at school on Monday didn't either. They all said huia were extinct. So frustrating. I could've taken a photo of the huia and been famous.

I know that the huia isn't extinct and when somebody else sees him, I'll turn around and tell Dad how right I am!

Sue Carpenter: Huia

The Sound of Silence

Ila Selwyn

my Titirangi bach fills with a proliferation of sounds
cars roll past, a motor bike roars up the road
an SUV swerves as it guns past the gate
buses chug up and down the narrow road
children chat on the walk home from school
a fledgling chirps in the garden seeking worms
a Tūī gargles in the Tōtara,
a Kererū plops, then flops as the Kahikatea settles
a Pīwakawaka flips and fans its tail as it swishes past

sounds proliferate in
my muffled mind
an empty house without my love
still sighs as its timbers dry out, snaps
contracts, during the heat of summer
doors, windows and gates expand with damp
groan, grumble and grate as I grabble
in the winter wet to open or close them

night- time fills with gentle muted sounds

rats or possums scratch on the roof

trees rustle in the wind outside my window

a branch blown by a blustery gale whacks the deck

the twang of a twig as it snaps under foot

the mournful morepork of a Ruru calling for its mate

its wing brushing through trees

as it searches for insects in the dark

hearing aids produce a pleasant sound

like water gently flowing

remove them and the sound

becomes a distant echo

when all else is quiet and gone to sleep

my breath goes steadily in and out

almost, but never, reaches

the sound of silence

The Old Bach

Ila Selwyn

our love-nest in Titirangi
sat on worn-out worm-eaten stumps
the flush toilet hung off one end
a long drop to the flax below

Peter jacks up our home with old bits of timber
builds two decks, digs out a basement, by hand
sets up a workplace with a potter's wheel
builds a top-hat brick kiln with an arched roof

our home starts to slip down the bank
Peter dismantles one deck, his workshop, stacks the timber
19 concrete piles later he rebuilds a bigger basement
a larger deck, a third kiln, the house grows

in 2019 the love of my life dies, our nest slips slightly
Peter's creative tiled entrance cracks under the strain
doors, windows and gates refuse to open or close
but our heart-broken home still hangs in there

A Few Tiny Poems

Ila Selwyn

an eiderdown of mist
lies lightly over the Manukau
the sun peeks through
feathers flutter, a sailboat appears

exercise on deck
pīwakawaka swoops, spins
flips, brushes my hair

pink sunrise bleeds to blue
 watercolour landscape

clouds dance in the sky
we foxtrot barefoot on grass
to an old boys' band

old tenacious toes and fibrous fingers
cling to soil, do their best to
hold the land together

Windswept

Marlene Milverton

Confessional

Alexandra Fraser

Sunday walk in the Waitaks
a processional into the bush
carrying day packs
with parkas
the weather uncertain
gingernuts juice
our communal snack

A nave stretches before us
shaded quiet
great perpendiculars
of buttressed kauri
columns of kahikatea
corbals of fungus
perching gargoyles epiphytes
 fan traceries of tree ferns
spiral fluting climbs rimu tōtara
clerestory of open branches
lets in roundels of light

We confess
the sin of asphalt and oil slick
The sin of the possum
and the evening bird's egg
the fire-scarred hills
the paddock the plough

We confess
the sin of the sub-division the mall
the smothering ginger
of the sweet seductive scent
the toxic waste
the rat and the stoat

We go to the bush to be made clean
our sins washed away with the rain

We hope to hear our absolution
in the wind
and in a faint kōkako call

Melissa Gunn: Epiphytes

Together

Sarah Valentine

They brought her home in a storm. Wind whipped through the boughs, branches cracked, the house snored through the gaps in the timber windows. She slept through it, milk-drunk with a full puku. When she woke next, the worst had passed. The percussive rustle and beat of the rain now a soothing white noise.

The tree survived the storm. Sure, it lost a few branches, but nothing hit the roof. The couple breathed a sigh of relief. The tree had stood since before her grandparents moved to Titirangi. It was a part of this place, a taonga. But those branches made them nervous.

The girl learned to climb when she was two. Crawled through the dog- door that was still there, though Bruno had died a decade ago. She was up the lowest branches of the tree when her dad found her. They were gone by morning - as high as her father could reach. Her mother cried quietly that night, patting her daughter's bum as she nodded off. But it was the right decision. It wasn't safe. The girl was seven when she found a way up again. One foot on the fence, pounce to the roof of the shed, then scramble and bump up on to the lowest hanging branch. She could see right over the Colemans' roof to the water. It winked at her and her laughter startled a tūī, who trilled an irritated song.

They were friends soon though. She built a birdhouse and climbed it nearly to the top, then filled the feeder with nectar. Her tree filled up with new friends.

The accident happened when she was twelve. Nearly too old to climb trees, anyway. Linda didn't think so, and they would climb together to feed the tūī. They liked to sit and watch the fishing boats, talking about things that would shock their whānau. The girl was the first to pull herself up to their branch that day, but it gave way. Linda's gasp slammed into the girl as the branches clawed past. The tūī fled as she fell. Her broken tailbone took months to heal. She was lucky the branch missed her skull. Linda decided they were too old to climb.

Her wedding happened in the backyard. Her father climbed the tree to string up the bunting. One foot on the fence, a shuffle on to the roof of the shed, and hauled his bulk up on the lowest branches. It groaned, but held firm. The fabric was her childhood clothes. Her mother had sewn them into neat triangles edged with pristine white. Tūī perched on the fabric and twittered through the ceremony. Her husband wondered why her tree was the only one filled with tūī. Did the others ever get lonely? The girl laughed. The wind whispered through the leaves of the tree, like it was sighing with pleasure.

It was close to two decades before she came home after that. The tree slowed its progress towards Ranginui, thirstier now in the summers. The whenua that had nurtured for so long now seem to be lacking in nutrients. It was like trying to suck smoothie through a soggy paper straw.

Less than two months after they returned, her parents died. One after another like they couldn't be apart. The woman made two small plaques and climbed them up her tree, her aging body grumbling and burning as she hauled herself higher. She had to wait, after she nailed them up, not having the strength to climb back down. That was okay though, the tūī kept her company.

They decided to stay. Moved back across the world to the house she had grown in. Their son visited sometimes, his accent too crisp for the summer heat.

"Why are so many of the leaves red?" he asked, and "is that fabric still there from your wedding?"

She just smiled and pointed out the kererū that had taken up residence. She wondered what had happened to her tūī.

She sat with the tree every day. Read her book under the branches, typed up accounts in the fresh air. Years meandered past as she slowed down. The ngahere had grown with her, the Waitākere Ranges breathing again after the logging a century ago. Her tree sat upon it like a tarnished crown, a giant that had survived it all. From her spot by its roots she felt the wind pick up and whip through the leathered leaves, then down through her lungs. She coughed so hard she passed out. When she came around she was confused. Had she been climbing and fallen again? Why was such a large branch beside her? Everything hurt, the bruises lasted weeks longer than they should have.

Her tree lost branch after branch.

Her body lost kilogram after kilogram.

Her husband carried her to her spot, tucked her up against the mighty trunk in her blanket. Her tiny body so small she needed its strength. She stroked the bleached bark, stared up through the skeletal branches. A single Tūī landed above her and she smiled.

There was a storm the night she died. The wind whipped through the boughs. The rain pelted down and lightning struck. There was a roar and a groan, a tremendous crack. She gasped, gurgled, felt his hand on her cheek, heard his whispers telling her he would be okay. Then she was gone.

The tree had missed the house when it fell. It was a miracle, everyone said so. He built her a coffin using wood from her tree, took her parents' plaques and laid them to rest with her. He scattered their ashes in the ngahere overlooking the Manukau, where they would grow again, together.

Titirangi (Performance Poem-Song)

Laurie Ross

Coming home to Titirangi in the evening
Driving into those sun-going-down hills
Sun-going-down hills, sun-going-down hills.
Making my way out of you, city
Wheeling away above you, city
To your golden skylight hori-zen.
Golden twilight-edge of heaven rising!

Coming home to Titirangi in the springtime
Kowhai tree blossoming and windchimes
Tinkle, tinkle, tinkle yellow
Hearing hello voices waiting for me
Man, and child – waiting for me in the wild.
Walking on down to the beach
Through the bush
Past your honey house
Your smoky funny house
Wandering along ocean's open arm
Dressed in lush native green
Magic is alive, the Fairy Queen survives
Birds and children fly between the trees
Men are growing in between the trees
Man grow, mangrove with your trees – please
Tree hands, tree hair, tree head, tree hips
Tree arms, tree feet, tree legs, tree lips – Tree Man!

Coming home to Titirangi in the summer
Ginger flowers flowering again
Flowering flowers in the rain
Lightly fragrancing the air
Sing and sing and sing and sing the air
So clear – up here – the air!
Grow on, flow on all you people
With your minds through the mist
Your misty twisty misty minds
Fog unfolds, clouds reveal the sun
Shining through radiant crystal water world
Sun shining through greenstone eyes
Green stoned highs, green stone IIIsss.

Hut Party

Melissa Gunn

"Don't leave too late. You don't want to be walking that track for the first time in the dark."

I barely acknowledged the club captain's warning. Of *course* I wouldn't be walking at night. I'd go to my last lecture and drive to the start of the track with a couple of hours daylight to spare. Plenty of time to meet the group at the hut. And my pack was ready to go, my boots tied on to it, ready to switch for my city sandals.

The lecture ran late. My car was towed. The sun… set.

Dithering at the start of the track, I double checked the locks and switched on my head torch. Should I risk it? Everyone else would be at the hut already. The track couldn't be that hard to follow at night, right?

My booted feet slipped on unseen clay. I tripped on roots lying wait in the darkness. Mud from a dozen slips coated my knees and backside. Something growled in the bushes ahead and I froze, foot in the air. Were there pigs in this part of the Ranges? Was it better to stride forward singing aloud or tiptoe back the way I had come? No-one would hear my cries if I was attacked. Fear-sweat dampened my merino t-shirt.

I'd come so far, and the track back would be just as slippery. A ruru's call beckoned me forward. Wouldn't it have flown away from danger? I walked on, holding my breath, hedging my bets. Wētā chittered in the trees. The moon rose, glinting on damp leaves and standing pools of water beside the track.

Distant music and laughter threaded through the sounds of the bush. My headtorch pierced the darkness and snagged on the wooden walls of the club hut.

Party time.

Jenny Clay: Tree ferns

Roaring 4Os, Piha

Philip Khouri

It was elemental.
Sun, tide and waves.
For two days we faced the sea
and turned our backs
to the complexity of the land.

Two days
divided into intervals
of wetsuits and wax.
Spotters called the colours.
Roachie called the heats.
We took turns at judging.
Monique recorded the results.

We almost burst our hearts
paddling to catch three waves in 15 minutes.
We grew gills
as the sun arced across the sky
and blinded our salt-stung eyes
in the afternoon.

By Sunday evening we were stuffed.
Waterlogged.
Piha had worked its magic
and smoothed away our sharp edges.

We ate dinner quietly.
Prizes were given
to the sound of laughter.
Barnett Hall was filled
with happy men and women.
Old friends new friends
sweetened by the sun
tumbled by the waves
and glowing.

Susan Glamuzina: Wild west coast

Midlife

Matt Niederer

Stones shifting under my weight
On the path to the tattoo studio
Buried in the Waitākere hills
Reminds me of Ōpanuku Stream
Born in the same bush
Where I swam as a child
Flowing smoothly past young kauri groves
Easing creases from rock
While the waterfall waits ahead
Gravity and current
Free fall into the pool

I plunge into the studio

Shrouded in weathered wood and greenstone

Carefully carved

We discuss my tattoo

A large kookaburra

I ask myself why?

Ask the stream why it flows

Swept along by my decision

The artist lays out pots of ink

Blue, green, black

His needle hums to life

I sink into the chair

The calm waters

At the base of the falls

Half in shadow, half in sun

They freeze on my skin

Still I dive under

The shock piercing

My lungs burn as I break the surface

Feet finding purchase

On the old stones beneath

Close-up

Jenny Clay

Dream of Titirangi

Angela Reading

On heaven's fringe midst the forest

I rest my body my mind my soul

It is to be my last home

Kept safe by my family protectors

Surrounding me with their love

I walk the footsteps of artists past

I feel their aura lingering around corners

I see their thoughts along a western coastline

Changing moods of broody sea and sky

Then clear bright days so fresh so bright

When a spectacular morning fiery orange sun rises

Then stares out from a Pacific Blue sky

When thunder and lightning flash

It does its worst to alienate the strong

And intimidate the weak

The kauri trees so straight like soldiers stand tall

The rimu hangs its head

Food and drink to artists eyes

So many shades of green

Just around the corner a splash of yellow glistens golden

Or even a magical group of purple wisteria

Will appear for a few days and then just be confetti

On the brown sodden earth beneath it

Susan Glamuzina: Nurseryweb

Kauri

Mels Barton

Kauri are special trees. They are some of the largest and longest-lived trees in the world and they retain vast amounts of carbon for thousands of years. Kauri are from an ancient lineage of Gondwanaland conifer trees that go back to the time of the dinosaurs, 250 million years ago. There are more than twenty different species of kauri around the south Pacific, of which the Aotearoa New Zealand species *Agathis australis* is the most southerly and the largest.

Kauri are a keystone species that support an entire ecosystem of 17 other species unique to kauri forests, plus many more that also occur in other ecosystems. They are ecosystem engineers that change their environment to suit themselves, stripping the nutrients from the soil to produce a kauri podsol. This is a specific soil-type where only those species that have evolved to thrive can survive alongside kauri.

To Māori, kauri are ancestors (tūpuna) and treasures (tāonga) that are revered. Surveys of landowners with kauri show people of all cultures express caring and a sense of awe for these trees. Kauri are special trees that invoke an emotional response in us all - and this is a good thing - because kauri are in big trouble.

When European settlers arrived in Aotearoa New Zealand kauri forests covered most of the northern third of the North Island, with forests of the giant trees clothing the hills from the ridgetops to the sea. What a sight that must have been! Unfortunately, the economic potential of this vast resource meant that within 100 years few forests were left. The kauri were stripped from the land and the timber exported to build the cities of Sydney, Melbourne and San Francisco as well as Auckland, Wellington and the rest. Now only 1% of original unlogged kauri forest remains, and only 3% has regenerated.

These remnants are fragmented into many small pockets of bush in gullies and on ridges, much on private land and iwi land, with the occasional larger stand in forests like the Waitākere Ranges (Te Wao Nui a Tiriwa / The Great Forest of Tiriwa), Waipoua and Puketi Forests and the Hunua Ranges. The fragmentation of these once large forests enables incursions of weeds, pests, and further damage from wind, and human activity. These, together with soil disturbance and compaction. affect the health of kauri and therefore threaten their survival.

However, there is a further existential threat to kauri that arrived in Aotearoa New Zealand at some point in the last few hundred years in the form of a deadly soil-borne pathogen that is causing kauri dieback disease. We do not know how it got here, when it arrived, or where it has come from, but we do know that it kills almost every kauri tree that it infects. There is no documented evidence so far of resistant trees, or recovery after infection without chemical treatment with phosphite, despite an intensive research project at the Forest Research Institute Scion, investigating resistance. This pathogen is a member of a genus called *Phytophthora* which comprises hundreds of soil-borne plant pathogens that have caused many devastating plant diseases around the world. Examples are the potato blight in Ireland (*Phytophthora infestans*), sudden oak death in California (*Phytophthora ramorum*) and jarrah dieback in western Australia (*Phytophthora cinnamomi*).

Phytophthora cinnamomi, in particular, is very widespread globally and is devastating many native species as well as agricultural crops. In Aotearoa New Zealand it is widespread, along with many other species of *Phytophthora*, and infects avocado. While it also affects kauri, it isn't usually fatal to kauri, unlike the pathogen causing kauri dieback disease.

The first clue of something affecting kauri came in 1972 when forest researcher Dr Peter Gadgill noticed dead and sick trees in a site he was studying on Aotea Great Barrier Island. He took samples and identified what he thought was *Phytophthora heveae*, but unfortunately advised the Auckland Regional Authority that it didn't appear to be very virulent because there were healthy trees within the stand. However, he did send samples of the pathogen to be stored at Kew Gardens in London, which turned out to be a really important decision.

Decades later in 2003, plant pathologists Dr Ross Beever and Dr Ian Horner started investigating dying kauri in Waipoua and Trounson Forests in Northland, and the potential role of *Phytophthora*.Later, in 2006, entomologist Dr Peter Maddison, noticed dead and dying kauri on the Maungaroa Ridge in Piha in the Waitākere Ranges. He notified Dr Beever, who investigated the site with Dr Horner and they linked the disease to an undescribed species of *Phytophthora*. Working with his research assistant, Dr Nick Waipara, Dr Beever wondered if it was the same one that Dr Gadgill had found, so they contacted Kew Gardens, obtained the samples and bingo - a match. They observed that it wasn't *Phytophthora heveae*, but a new species. Temporarily named *Phytophthora Taxon Agathis* (PTA) it was eventually named *Phytophthora agathidicida* (meaning "plant destroyer, kauri killer").

This discovery started a chain of events that was frustratingly slow when serious action needed to be taken to prevent the spread of the disease in Auckland, especially in the Waitākere Ranges. Instead, Auckland became an unfortunate battleground between conservation and recreation interests.

Within the Waitākere Ranges was a rabbit warren of over 250 km of poorly-maintained walking tracks, mainly comprising mud and tree roots and occasional patches of gravel. The majority of the forest was regrowth, having been extensively logged right through to the 1930s, with some small patches of unlogged primeval bush. These include the Cascades, the heart of the park and which had been preserved as the core of the Auckland Centennial Memorial Park. This was the precursor to what we now know as Waitākere Ranges Regional Park.

In 2006, the regional parks were managed by the Auckland Regional Council, but in 2010 amalgamation of the regional, district and city councils resulted in a single unitary authority called Auckland Council. This massive upheaval in the region's local governance resulted in a more commercial and urban-focused model, under which the Council's Biosecurity team, led by Jack Craw, did its very best to put in place a 5-yearly rolling monitoring programme surveying kauri health across all the parks in the entire region.

This included a network of shoe-cleaning stations around the track network and the closure of a few key tracks. Unfortunately, having such a muddy, poorly maintained track network, combined with over 2 million visitors per year, the continued spread of this soil borne disease was inevitable. The first kauri health survey of the Waitākere Ranges in 2011 showed that an average of 8% of kauri were infected or showing symptoms of disease. The survey was undertaken by a helicopter flying a grid pattern across the entire park and identifying trees with canopy dieback.

These sites were then investigated by a ground truthing team taking soil samples and recording symptoms. When the survey was repeated in 2016 the results showed that the incidence of disease had doubled, with 19% of kauri showing symptoms. The symptomatic trees were most closely associated with the track network, waterways and predator control bait lines. It was clear that people were the main vector of the disease in the Waitākere forest.

This news horrified conservation groups and Te Kawerau ā Maki, mana whenua for Te Wao Nui a Tiriwa. Te Kawerau saw the disease as an existential threat, not only to the forest, but also to them. They immediately approached Auckland Council and requested that the Regional Park tracks be closed to prevent further spread of the disease. Despite strong support for the iwi from influential conservation groups such Forest & Bird, The Tree Council, the Waitākere Ranges Protection Society and the Friends of Regional Parks, the Council argued such a move would be impossible to enforce. The Mayor at the time stated publicly that it would take "armed guards and razor wire" to close the Regional Park.

Te Kawerau ā Maki were not prepared to take no for an answer and on 2 December 2017 they placed a rāhui, or customary prohibition, over the entire forested area of Te Wao Nui a Tiriwa, asking for the public to stay out of the forest, respect the rāhui and allow the forest to heal. And so began the rāhui campaign...

The conservation groups stood with the iwi and publicly stated their support for the rāhui, calling for the public to stand together with them. There was a huge outpouring of public support, stoked by the media who were delighted to have such a controversial topic to cover during the dead zone for news over the extended summer holiday period. There were endless news articles, TV programmes, radio interviews and public meetings. Representatives from

Te Kawerau ā Maki, Forest & Bird, The Tree Council, the Waitākere Ranges Protection Society and the Friends of Regional Parks were constantly fronting public debates, doing interviews and giving talks. The rāhui was the hot topic of conversation at every party, BBQ and dinner table that Christmas.

While there was opposition, particularly from some of the tramping clubs and some tourism companies and accommodation providers, there were some critical supporters that swung the pendulum of support in favour of doing the right thing. The manager of the Whatipū Lodge and campground, Wayne McKenzie, refused to take bookings from anyone doing the Hillary Trail, the multi-day hike around the coastline of the Waitākere Ranges, and along which many of the infected trees were located. The organiser of the Hillary Trail Marathon, Shaun Collins of Lactic Turkey, cancelled the 2018 marathon and told his 20,000-strong Facebook community, that he was respecting the rāhui. The University of Auckland, among many other academic institutions, refused to take students out into the Ranges.

Public support kept increasing and by the time the Auckland Councillors were back at their desks in early 2018 they realised they needed to be seen to take positive action. On 20 February 2018 the councillors, led by Deputy Mayor Penny Hulse and Mayor Phil Goff overturned their previous decision and voted overwhelmingly (by 20 votes to 1) to close both the Waitākere Ranges and Hunua Ranges Regional Parks to prevent further spread of kauri dieback disease.The Ministry for Primary Industries followed up the Council decision by placing Controlled Area Notices over any tracks that subsequently re-opened, requiring people to use the cleaning stations and stick to the track, or face prosecution.

This was a huge victory for Te Kawerau ā Maki and their supporters Forest & Bird, The Tree Council, the Waitākere Ranges Protection Society and the Friends of Regional Parks, but also for the people of Auckland. In closing the Hunua Ranges, which are still free of the disease, they have protected healthy kauri ecosystem for future generations.

The closures created huge political pressure to find the money to upgrade the track infrastructure to make it safe to reopen the tracks. Te Kawerau ā Maki and Auckland Council agreed that when tracks were upgraded and effective cleaning stations installed at all entry points, then the rāhui could be lifted from those individual tracks and the public could use them again. This was the start of constructive collaboration between the iwi and the Council that has been a template for successful co-management. In 2018 Auckland Council consulted with ratepayers who supported a Natural Environment Targeted Rate collected to deliver $100 million in additional funding over 10 years to protect kauri health and upgrade the track infrastructure. Today in 2025 the track upgrade programme is almost complete and the very last section of the Hillary Trail at Zion Hill should be completed this year.

The new tracks are of very high quality boxed gravel, boardwalks and steps and are constantly audited to ensure they maintain a dry-foot standard so that people are not spreading soil-borne pathogens along the tracks. So, all good for the walkers, but what about the infected kauri?

There is still no cure for kauri dieback disease, but an effective treatment has been developed by Dr Ian Horner of Plant & Food Research. Adapting the phosphite treatment, used for decades in avocado orchards to control *Phytophthora cinnamomi*, he developed a treatment method for kauri infected with *Phytophthora agathidicida* that can keep them alive if applied early enough and repeated approximately every 5 years. Dr Horner reassessed his original trial plots after 10 years and found most of the trees were still alive after a single treatment, while many of the untreated trees around them continued to decline and die. This treatment system has been applied by a community trust called Kauri Rescue, which was started by a team of scientists, iwi and community representatives initiated by Dr Horner. Kauri Rescue has been working with private landowners and iwi to treat infected trees on their properties and monitor the health responses of the trees over time. Since 2017, Kauri Rescue Trust has helped landowners and iwi to treat and monitor over 3500 trees. Initially funded by the Biological Heritage National Science Challenge, Kauri Rescue Trust is now supported by a range of funders, including Auckland Council via the Natural Environment Targeted Rate. On public land, however, there has been very little treatment of infected kauri and trees continue to die. There was an initial treatment of around 10,000 trees at Piha where the infection was first noticed in 2006, but this has not been repeated or expanded to treat other areas. The Cascades is one of the most heavily infected areas and these trees are now in a critical state of poor health. Kauri Rescue worked with Te Kawerau ā Maki in 2024 to treat a small number of the largest trees in the Cascades, as part of a large-tree treatment trial led by Dr Horner, but this is yet to be expanded to other trees and areas in the park.

The iwi and conservation groups continue to work together to lobby Auckland Council and the government to take stronger action on kauri dieback. In 2022, more than 16 years since the discovery of the disease in Piha, a National Pest Management Plan and kauri dieback management agency, Tiakina Kauri (part of the Ministry for Primary Industries), was enacted by legislation. This national plan requires landowners and agencies, such as councils and the Department of Conservation, to monitor and report the disease and take positive action to prevent its spread and protect healthy kauri. One of its primary functions is to enable iwi to protect kauri within their own rohe (tribal areas). The battle for kauri that began in Waitākere spread across the country and has resulted in legislative change. It took far too long, but we got there in the end, and everyone who took action to respect the rāhui should be proud of what has been achieved. The lesson shown to us by Te Kawerau ā Maki that leading by example and doing the right thing, despite overwhelming obstructions, pays huge dividends. Continuing this leadership role, Te Kawerau have recently launched their proposed Heart of the Ngahere Strategy, a 1000-year plan to protect the still healthy centre of the Waitākere Ranges for future generations. The plan has been supported by Auckland Council and the conservation groups that continue to stand with Te Kawerau to protect kauri and enhance the mauri (life force) of Te Wao Nui a Tiriwa (Waitākere Ranges).

Finally, 17 years after the Waitākere Ranges Heritage Area Act was passed, on 14 August 2025 Auckland Council agreed to enter into a Deed of Acknowledgement with Te Kawerau ā Maki and the Crown. Auckland Council also agreed to recommend that, once the Deed is signed by all parties, the Governing Body establish a joint committee of council that will develop and implement a strategic plan for the Waitākere Ranges Heritage Area. This formal recognition of Te Kawerau ā Maki's association with the area and their place on a joint committee to better manage the area is an historic moment and the event was witnessed by a full council chamber, overflowing with members of Te Kawerau ā Maki and their supporters.

Kauri Melody

Edna Heled

Boardwalk

Jordan Hanna

Walking up to the look out, sun shining down on me
I hear wind rustling the tree
Tūī chirping in the distance
cicadas buzzing around
the scent of nature coming from every direction
feeling the wood of the railing under my fingers
as I'm looking over the edge
I see trees all around covering the ground below
ocean in the distance as blue as the sky with boats sailing
enjoying the beautiful day.

Myth or Legend

Karen Morris-Denby

Deep in the ranges
a long time ago
mysterious sounds echoed
bright lights would glow

The very first settlers
some historians say
the Patupaiarehe (bush fairies)
often hid through the day

They grew healthy crops
sang beautiful tunes
planting their vegetables
following the phases of the moon

Their perfectly kept hair
blonde and curly
they always began work
before sunrise so early

Their blue eyes shone
when catching fish from the sea
taking what they needed
the children were never hungry

Peaceful loving creatures
they never knew wars
as they weaved fishing nets
along the beach shores

Then came the warriors
who wanted their land
grabbing everything they
wanted in their cold cruel hands

Returning on the full moon
Patuapaiarehe trembled with fright
as they were never taught
how to stand up and fight

They were butchered
and roasted in roaring fires
most were eaten even though
many were still alive

The warriors stole their culture
their souls and their pride
some say it is a myth
others a legend to hide

Betwixt

Tania Leigh Pauling

Grace

Fiona d'Young

Gentle visitor to our shores

We tend your memory like a precious garden

An exquisite flower, newly bloomed

Your life force has joined with our whenua

We carry you on and forward as our own

Gone, but never forgotten

Waitākere remembers you

With aroha

Always

Five Haiku, Waitākere Series

Suzanne Weld

Ngahere beckons
Sun on lush foliage
beams healing green light.

Soft trail underfoot
Strong rhythm of earth's heartbeat
The land is alive.

Riroriro trill
Tap, tapping of droplets
Streams sing in the rain.

Pungent, earthiness
Wafting tī kōuka fragrance
Ngahere exhales.

Drink in a river
Savour cascades, wairua
of Waitākere.

Bougainvillea on Otititori Bay Rd

Di Nash

round a corner
and there it is
a fountain, a cascade
a waterfall of frothing purple
a hundred feet high
faces you with its beauty
takes your breath away

Melissa Gunn: Toropapa (Alseuosmia): sweet scented flower of the understory.

Get Away

Lee Simpson

I booked the Waitākere retreat for one, on a holiday homes site. Two nights in the middle of nowhere, but only half an hour away from Auckland city. No devices, no drama, no work calls, two days of only me.

I parked at the designated spot and saw a track with the words '*Get away retreat*' on them. I grabbed a bag of clothes in one hand and my handbag in the other, locked the car and walked up the path and around the corner and up twenty steps and around another corner. I kept climbing up and the house was nowhere in sight. I still had five more bags in the car. I climbed and climbed. Turned and climbed, until I finally saw a little shack, but the path ended at the shack. Surely this isn't it? I tried the key in the door, and opened it. There was a note welcoming me.

I looked around. There was a small fireplace, bed, desk, and a camping oven. Some blankets and cushions but nothing else. No toilet. No refrigerator. No oil, spices, or even spatula. I put my clothes down and looked out the window at the view. It was spectacular – however the sunlight was fading, and I had more gear to bring up, how would I even cook my chicken – let alone refrigerate it? I jogged down the steps and round the bends to the car and by the time I got there – typical Auckland weather – the clouds had dropped and were threatening rain. I gathered everything I could and put them into just four bags instead of the five. As I closed the boot the heavens opened, and I screamed as the water rushed over me faster than I thought possible.

A jogger ran towards me, 'Are you okay?'

'It's raining hard, hadn't expected it.'

'This rain is crazy – let me help you.'

'Those steps are murder,' I said, meaning no, I don't expect that.

'Well, I must help you now,' he winked.

We each grabbed two bags and ran up the steps and around, and up and around and up. By the time we got into the cabin we were drenched and frozen.

He unloaded his bags on the desk and looked at me awkwardly.

'The rain's bound to stop soon. Do you want to wait and dry off?' I said. His smile somehow filled his face, widest and brightest smile I'd seen, and it was highlighted with big brown eyes.

I tried to light the fire, but it wouldn't spark. His first attempt was successful, and we both took off our outer layers of wet clothes waiting for the little room to warm up.

So, him just in boxer shorts and a T-shirt. Me in a singlet and bike shorts. Playing cards at the small desk. Bob wasn't into cards; he kept looking outside. I was meant to be here alone – finding myself, but in the presence of Bob I heard myself laugh for the first time this year, my shoulders relaxed. I didn't need to be alone, I was always alone, putting pressure on myself. I needed to find company – someone who relaxed me, help me unwind.

'The rain is not easing up,' he said – 'we should climb in the hot spa in the rain.'

'Absolutely, what a great idea.' I would never have thought of that. We embraced the rain, overlooking the view of the bush as the sun set.

My clothes disappeared. The darker it got, the closer I got to Bob. Our fingers intertwined. Darker. Our chests pressed upon each other. Darker. Lips explored. Dark.

I definitely didn't need time alone. I needed to remind myself that I was alive and my body had never pulsed faster. I let go of my expectations of myself and let myself be free.

Susan Glamuzina: Bush steps

Driving West

Piers Davies

Beyond
any kaleidoscope –
 a lexicon of
shades of green
multiplies shining
fresh beneath the clouds
rolling high above
the ridges and folds
of this shimmering
landscape.

Ranges

63

Marlene Milverton

Mesmerised by Kitekite Falls

Denise O'Hagan

It's a long way up
you tumble down
polishing rocks
a never-ending shower
of moving shroud
that moss collects
as you slide and glide
that glistens and shimmies
alive, a moving tide
of luscious green and white

we abide your beauty
your natural wealth
your gift to us
not asked for, just dealt
air that breathes of freshness
of lush bush and green
a waterfall,
nature's own true scheme

Sue Gee: Opal pools, kawakawa and nikau

Te Ana Ru

Bog Bakaric

Steve took a sigh and looked away from the ferry as he walked the wharf boardwalk on the side of Paratutae Island, from Wonga Wonga Bay and over onto Whatipū beach. This was his rest, and although he would be paid a small koha to play, the trombone was his passion.

He had a natural musical gift and had learnt to play well in the Army brass band in his teens. Stopping, he placed his trombone case and luggage on the ground and took his pipe from inside his finely tailored black penguin suit jacket. He had kept the case as well maintained as he could over the years. It had survived the torturous voyage from Europe to New Zealand, the gum fields in the far north and the many locations around the North Island he had worked. There was a large scratch on the side, which he had attempted to buff out and polish with shoe polish. This reminded him not of the slight fall that caused it, but rather the long-ago dance with his Dalmatian band mates, high on an isolated hill overlooking Dargaville on a St Peter's day.

His musical talent had made him welcome and break through the English- only barriers. His performances had opened doors and forged connections, which led to work.

He'd been a stone mason, heavy haulage and earthworks worker on many significant projects after his time in the gumfields. It now had him playing to the youth of Auckland's elite tonight in the Te Ana Ru caves otherwise known as The Ballroom.

A man's voice called out to the band members. 'Your tents are set up at the Gibbons house, if you'd please follow me.'

Steve hurried through the familiar ritual of tapping, filling and lighting the pipe with perfect fluidity, before picking up his bag and instrument case. As they walked along the stream side to the Whatipū homestead of the Gibbons, Steve talked with the band members, his English polished despite his heavy accent, he concentrated as he always did when speaking English. Not so much on actual language, but to speak well like an Englishman to ensure he could be accepted.

The conversation was of old wars and unrest again in Europe, but then shifting to politics. Steve was sure not to talk of war politics, and cautious about speaking ill of others, including famous people, for he had learnt that such conversations were often turned against his countrymen as 'outsiders'. He felt the conversation too formal and too heavy. He took one last puff of the pipe, tapped it out and placed it in his pocket with his free hand. Pulling on his charismatic wit, he spontaneously broke into song. His rich, operatic voice was an excellent icebreaker, lightening the mood quickly. In perfect English, he sang part of the comedic H.M.S Pinafore opera he had learnt off a sailor on his way to New Zealand. When he finished, the other band members and passengers from the boat further down the track clapped, requesting more. He obliged, standing to the side of the track continuing to sing as the next huddle of passengers filed past towards the Gibbons Homestead.

At the Homestead, the band were assisted by young men to get their equipment down a track which wound to Te Ana Ru caves while the other passengers were fed. A heavy mat took the sand off Steve's boots as he wiped them and once inside the cave, he could only admire the beauty of the venue. The cave had been arranged with ribbons of multiple colours draped across the roof. The kauri board dance floor was pristinely polished. Beautiful kerosene lanterns lit where the band sat, while oil lanterns and candles were set on the remainder of the cave walls.

A short while later food and wine was brought to the band members by young men accompanied by an older man in his forties. The older man's skin was bronze, his skin well weather worn and lips looked dry and about to crack, but he looked solid, fit and otherwise looked healthy. He laid out the order of the evening and basic rules for the band members, before he sat on a chair he had pulled to the middle of the cave. 'Look...' said the man.

'We are having this dance tonight on a sacred night. Don't be alarmed by what I tell you. It is only during the Pink Moon and probably only time these dances fall on this time of the year, however....'

The man sighed before continuing.

'You will be last up, so I need to be clear on some rules that need to be followed for your safety.

One, you are not to swim in the water, whether it be the creek, river or sea, no matter exceptions and who asks you to.

Two, if you hear your name called by someone you know is not here, you didn't. Three, if you heard a noise that doesn't match the location, you didn't, don't go and investigate.

Four, do not walk alone.

Five, if you hear something following you, you didn't.

Six, if you think you are being followed or hear something following you, do not run, remember there are no large predators here.

Seven, stay on the track, there is no need to go up high, in the hills or climb the rocks and cliffs.

Eight, beware the wahine. She will appear in hazy form, and is mute, but that doesn't diminish her danger.

You will be fine, young men, just stay safe and take no risks tonight.' As soon as these words were uttered, there was a cold breeze into the entrance of the cave. The candles and lamps simultaneously flickered, and a light fog rolled downward from above.

Steve looked at his band mates. Jimmy, the Irish cello player, smiled and said, 'My goodness lads,' before cracking a few jokes.

The evening progressed. The fog outside the cave thickened but inside the festivities and dancing continued. A table full of food and drinks was kept replenished and glasses were constantly topped up by waiting staff. The band played endlessly with great fanfare and delight. The cave provided the perfect ambience and acoustics, the polished floor a dramatic and beautiful contrast to the black sand and darkness outside. The numerous candles and oil lamps cast a heavenly light over the evening.

At 3am a bell was rung. The dance floor was still half full and music lively, an energy that started and emanated throughout the night and early morning from the band.

Steve was the last to pack up, having helped everyone else first. As the courteous man he was, he walked last in a long single-file line towards the tents by the homestead.

"Stepe, Stepe," he could have sworn his sister called from behind. She was in Europe, and no one called him by this name in Aotearoa. He looked back. The fog was thick, but he saw the outline of a girl in a pink dress. He walked towards her. She had straight black hair and skin that glowed bronze in the moonlight. She smelt earthy, of wildflowers and Mānuka oil. She seemed to glide as she walked to him, and silently slid her cold hand into his. Reaching up, she kissed him gently with icy lips, then turned him back down the track to walk towards the cave. Steve was transfixed by her beauty, her skin slightly illuminating the darkness and thick fog. She didn't speak, and he simply followed.

They walked past the cave still illuminated by the candles and oil lamps, then further along the path towards the beach. He pulled on her hand to turn towards to the cave. He thought of taking her back to the homestead. As she turned to face him, her eyes shimmered like pāua shell in the moonlight. A high-pitched sound came screeching from the cave, and a stampede of heavy footsteps came thumping over the sandy path. Her face contorted with terror, and her hand still gripping Steve's, she ran for the ocean.

Steve remembered the Pink Moon rules, almost too late. He ran with her, trying to keep up as the noise grew louder.

Susan Glamuzina: Cave

Spoil - a Haiku Sequence

Amanda Eason

Farming with a match.
Settlers have no idea.
The Pākehā way -

Scraped hills shift and fall.
Mud choked rivers lift and slow.
Our inheritance.

The last huia
gone for hats and museums.
How much was it worth?

Racing for kauri
logs spill downstream to the coast.
Prized masts for tall ships.

Gold, gum, trees, birds – land.
Lads, sign up – make your fortune!
Be quick – while it lasts!

Why forest the berm?
Cut grass is a poor excuse.
My men had axes.

Scraped hills shift and fall.
Mud choked rivers lift and slow.
Our inheritance.

when you were around

Alexandra Balm

In the days when you were here
the sun shone its morning light on the hill
(against a mountain of glossy leaves)
in front of my window

the sky concurred – its clear blue
as hopeful as an infant's gaze

we walked to the river
and dipped our feet in its cold waters
on midsummer night;
we made bedstraw wreaths
and let them float downstream –
tea candles in their centre –
towards a future of hope.

In the days when you were still here

all was right with the world,

though I never knew it

at the time

when joy pervaded the world

invincible

Promise

Alexandra Balm

One day we'll have completed
the quest that we have started
and all the years of pushing the boulder
uphill, of holding the thread
through maze-like
ombre et penombre
lived through, expressed or merely hinted at
(against sparks of timidly affirming,
half-believed provisional triumphs)
wouldn't have been
in vain

We would have proved
the proof's not always
in the destination of the pudding,
the crowning of one's life –,
tidal *corsi e ricorsi* –,
the process of every day
becoming

You, Again

Alexandra Balm

i haven't heard from you in a while
How is it going there, behind the veil,
across the woods and mountains?
Do you continue as usual, awaiting another
life? Do you dream-remember this one
left here – wide open books of filtered,
sublimated experience?

Do you visit the dreams and reveries
of your family, of close friends, of enemies
– who hasn't got them –
that didn't quite matter in the end?

i haven't heard from you in a while, but i have your words
– my brain waves shape themselves to converse with them,
as spirit to spirit, emanation to emanation, vibration to vibration.

This night that I inhabit (it's past midnight)
and that engulfs me
like a cloud of mist-grace in Muriwai,

this night where I feel at home –
is it part of your new, expanded
being?

Sue Gee: 49 Shades of Grey

The Mummy

Ashley Lindsay

The mummy lay, motionless on the gravel path. Like she'd toppled out of the back of a truck on her way to the museum. But there was no way a truck could get out here, by the flowing river in Huia. Surrounded by bush and the perfect amount of swirling fog. Cream bandages wrapped tight around her body, the ends frayed and splayed out under the moonlight. She was completely covered, except for her face—pale and whiter than the bandages that bound her.

She was probably freezing cold. My own coveralls and boots weren't enough to ward off the below-freezing air. My dark hair was tied back and tucked under a hairnet. I wished it was a beanie. Or at least something warmer.

The crime-scene was roped off, and the area outside it was bustling with activity. Cops. Detectives. Witnesses. Camera men. And Ana and I — forensics.

"Here, Mel," Ana said, handing me one of those plastic numbers you see on CSI. She had a thick, eastern European accent and her face, like mine, was covered with a mask. I took the yellow-plastic five from her with a gloved hand. "Just put it where some evidence might be," she continued.

"Right," I whispered, intimidated by the flood lights illuminating us, the people scrutinising me, the mummy lying motionless on the path, and the immense forest. Usually, this place would be masked in darkness, alone at this time of night. But we were disturbing its slumber.

"And use these," she passed me a petri-dish and some tweezers, "to gather what you can."

I nodded and surveyed the empty ground in front of me. Detritus, sticks, and fine gravel.

"And act like you know what you're doing," she said with a chuckle. "Especially when Detective Greenwood comes past." She pointed to a suit- clad, beanpole of a man who stood with a few police officers sipping take- away coffee. "If he asks you anything, just nod. Don't say anything or you'll get us into trouble."

I nodded.

"See, you're a natural," Ana said. She looked up as a hush came over the crime-scene. Detective Greenwood and his cops had set down their coffees and strode as a pack back to their police cars. The cameramen moved into position. And Ana whispered, "Showtime."

The crime-scene was silent. Except for the crunching of Detective Greenwood's boots. He walked purposely towards the mummy talking to another cop. "We found her like this," the cop was saying. I pretended to be busy, urging my numb fingers to work the tweezers and gather some leaves in my petri dish as Detective Greenwood approached.

"You wouldn't expect a mummy out here," the Detective commented as he lifted the crime-scene tape and marched towards the mummy. "Do we know how she got here yet?"

"Not yet," the cop said. "We'll know more once forensics finishes their analysis."

The detective looked over at Ana and me. I put my head down; my breath swirled around my face in the winter air as I peered down at the gravel underfoot. Searching. Well, acting like I was searching.

"Found anything?" I knew he was directing the question at me. I looked up at him, met his steely grey eyes, and nodded, doing my best impression of a forensic scientist.

"There's some interesting drag marks," Ana said, "but no obvious signs of the cause of death. Once we get her back to lab and remove the bandages, we might have a better idea." Ana was standing over the body with an air of authority about her. "Poor girl," Ana added, shaking her head. "No one deserves to die like this."

"It's a strange one, that's for sure," Detective Greenwood remarked. He pulled out his notepad and jotted a few things down. "Keep me posted if you find anything," the Detective said as he crouched down to get a better look at the victim. He held his position, peering closely at the wrapped body for a few seconds before—

"And, end scene!" a loud voice called out. Immediately the crime-scene filled with noise as the film crew rushed forward. The detective stood up and made his way off set. He was quickly robed in a puffer jacket and led to his heated trailer.

The mummy sat up, shivering. "It's bloody freezing," she muttered as some of the film crew wrapped her in a fleece blanket and handed her a steaming cup of coffee. "Good work people," the director said. "Let's do another take. This time, with more atmosphere." He looked towards the people manning the fog machine who began pumping more fog into the still air. "I want it to feel... eerier. And we need more light," he called out. "Our mummy has too much shadow."

"Extras," the assistant director said, looking at the cops. "Do exactly what you did the first time. It's looking great. Maybe you," he pointed at the tallest cop, "can lift the tape for our detective when he passes by. And forensics," he directed his gaze at Ana and I, "I want more movement. Pace around the scene, drop some of those plastic number thingys, bag some evidence. Do more of whatever forensic scientists do."

"What do you think about having the newbie come up closer to the body? Seems more realistic to have the two of us collecting evidence there?" Ana asked.

The assistant director paused for a second. "Do what you think is best," he said before moving on to talk to some of the other extras posing as witnesses. Ana crouched down, reached into her forensics box, and handed me a stack of numbers and some more evidence bags. "Place these around the body," Ana said, "but make sure you move out of the way when the camera pans around

to focus on me and the Detective when I say my lines." "Right and—" I began to say.

"Places," the director yelled out. "Let's make this take the last one so our poor mummy doesn't get hypothermia."

The film crew removed the blanket from the mummy, snatched her coffee away, and cleared the scene. The mummy sighed and said, "I'm not getting paid enough for this." She gave me an exasperated look before lying down on the gravel to act dead.

Susan Glamuzina: Flow

One Evening

Jenny Clay

in the backyard
in the bush
it gets darker

through tree shadows
shivers of light
a kitchen

and a full blue moon
dappled yellow circle
watching
from above

I cling to tree trunks on
 the way down
the slope

no clear footholds
in root and bare earth
recently slick with rain

I reach the house
turn on more lights
grab a broom
to sweep
the green wilted bougainvillea
leaves
from the path

there is a crunch underfoot

I did not tread lightly
I did not see you pūriri moth
the same shade as the leaves
your wings outstretched
your body flattened
such heavy feet

did you come with me
through the bush
or were you waiting here
for light and darkness
for camouflage
like the green

of the sweat shirt
I wore

how clumsily we tread

I scoop you up
and put you in the kitchen
beside the newly sprouted
flax seeds with their long floppy
leaves falling over
themselves

I can not apologise enough
for how clumsy
us humans are

but I can
write you a poem

Weaving Road

Susan Glamuzina

between two Huia

no huia to be seen

jumping fish

rods out

lures on

lures lost

lures on with more knots
jumpers on

seaweed caught

tide goes out

feet off the rocks

feet in the ocean

rods fly

seaweed caught

fish caught

fish lost

rods fly

sun moves

wind picks up

rods fly

no dinner

takeaways for tea

fish burgers and kumara chips

So Far Away

Suzanne Gee

At Karekare the earth is baked into a solid impermeable crust. In the heat, busy ants scurry over deep wide cracks. It's been a too long too hot summer. Drought has been declared in the North. Abundant mānuka flowers exude their subtle sweet scent, but no bees arrive to feast. In contrast, five years ago, my tiny lawn – a blanket of clover – vibrated and hummed with honey bees packing pollen on their legs. Today, mask wearing council contractors adjust hoses and nozzles. They spray and spray. Roadside weeds drip and glisten with pesticide.

Tī kōuka – cabbage tree. Your clusters of luscious berries weigh you down. Tauhou – silver eye, where are you? Come eat! Kawakawa – your fruits... orange, plump and juicy... waiting. Where are you Kererū? Come eat. Play your part. Disperse the seed. Where are you birds when the sun go down? You're so far away from me.

Mosquitoes – back then, how you tormented me. Now, in early evenings, my windows are open but you don't fly in.

What a conundrum. I don't miss you, but the ecosystem needs you. Summers ago, I remember black clouds. Hundreds and hundreds of swarming midges. Protein for the birds. Today, midges no more. In recent times, as a volunteer for an environmental group, the chill in the air and mist in the mornings were my signal to don a warm jacket, traipse so far away, two kilometers into te ngahere, Te Wao Nui a Tiriwa and reload bait stations with the anticoagulant brodifacoum – rats and stoats being the target predators. The gloves I put on were not protection against cold but protection against chemicals.

"Like all anticoagulants," AI tells me, "brodifacoum is highly toxic to humans, pets and other wildlife. It works by inhibiting production of vitamin K. Vitamin K is crucial for the synthesis of proteins required for blood clotting. The poison is absorbed into the liver. As the poisoned animal loses its ability to clot blood, internal bleeding occurs. Eventually, the poison leads to convulsions, organ damage, shock and death."

A long time ago, when I had newly moved to the Waitākeres, a little grey mouse came into my house. I thought it was cute. Sweet thing. How slowly it walked. All wobbly – kind of drunk. It fell forward and got up. I pulled up a chair to watch. It fell again, on its side this time, nose twitching, stomach quivering, its tail making slow loops on the carpet. What was I watching?

The days are getting shorter. Chill is not in the air. It should be. But it will soon be time again. Time to reload the bait stations. I survey those measured bags, blue pellets, the poison. We have a dog now. Secondary-poisoning is on my mind.

That poor little mouse. My existential crisis has arrived. Can I do it? I don't know. The Dire Straits ear-worm, You're so far...you're just so far away from me.

Sue Gee: Karekare Valley, Afternoon Tipple with Oranges and Krispie Biscuits

Whispers of the River Swing

Marco Glamuzina

Beneath the sky so vast and blue,
A quiet stream runs soft and true.
Its mirrored face reflects the trees,
That dance and murmur in the breeze.

A sturdy branch extends with grace,
Holding time in its embrace.
A rope swing sways in patient wait,
For one more soul to test its fate.

The echoes of a child's cheer,
Still linger in the atmosphere.
Barefoot steps on the mossy ground.
There is courage to be found.

The wind blows soft, the branches sigh,
A tūī drifts throughout the sky.
The rope swing sways, its job is clear
To cradle dreams, to cast out fear.

Perhaps one day when dusk is near,

A weary heart will wander here.

And with a breath a fleeting thought,

Remember joys the years forgot.

So come, take a swing.

Susan Glamuzina: Swing

Exhibition Drive

Raewyn Booth

Awake, walking along Exhibition Drive, the steps taken are real
My feet touch the new gravel that has been placed over deep scars below
Alive, the feeling that flows through me as I hear the song of the Tūī
calling to be heard by others that bask in the surrounding beauty
Sunlight peeks through the branches of trees
that have escaped the turmoil of being torn apart from nature's recent fury
Beauty surrounds the well-worn path that many have walked before.
The glistening of the ferns, the plants, the grasses,
the greenness is everywhere
It takes hold of me and enters my heart leaving sunshine
Awake, alive and beauty
This will always be Exhibition Drive

A Series of Haiku

Joel Ramos

I'm Waitākere
mountainous and beautiful
please come and see me

Susan Glamuzina

high pitched song
flitting tail gracefully
fanned sky dancers

Tonchi Glamuzina

tūī bumbles in tree
fantail zipping
waxeye hustling

Jordan Hanna

tūī chirping
wind rustling nurture
water calm below

Lucas Glamuzina

no wind in my hair
sun blazing from up above sea
breezes blow soft

Huia

Wolfgang B Sperlich

When you leave Titirangi Village
With an expensive latte in a paper cup
On your way to Huia
Deciding on the roundabout
Which way to go
Huia Road
Or
Woodlands Park Road
The latter off Scenic Drive
You suddenly remember
Having seen the Waitākere Ranges
From New Lynn
Buying groceries in the supermarket
It makes no sense
You think
All this colonial nonsense

There was a Lady from Lynn

Who drove to Huia

And she moved right in

On Upland Road

The surrounding misty peaks

Remind her of Norway

She collects feathers

Shed by tūī, pūkeko and huia

No no that was a long long time ago

Te Wao Nui a Tiriwa

But before you get to the Huia Lookout

There is a sign Te Rau-o-te-Huia

With the nicely painted huia bird

But some Pākehā historian

Tells her

Huia was named after a boat by the same name

Ferrying kauri logs

Oh how she hugs the kauri on her land

Please don't die

She drinks kawakawa tea

Talks to Otto the cat

Who is hiding under the bed

Because he is old and scared of birds

She worries about the grandkids in Woodlands Park and China

The siren goes off for the third time

Is it the start of WW III

Or

Another fire at Cornwallis

The beach she loves

Two wild ducks arrive

She names them Albert and Victoria

Her husband is German too

He's an anarchist and worries day and night

About ecocide and huia species extinction

So he planted an abundance of fruit trees

For the missing bird

He cuts back the harakeke to make room

For pōhutukawa, rimu and tōtara

Should she jump in the car

Drive to Whatipū

Or

Rearrange the greenhouse flowers

She doesn't know if she's coming or going

Only the painted huia knows

Barbara Peterson: Framed Ranges

Green

Susan Glamuzina

Mix green
lighter
darker
add yellow
next white
black
swiping round
then anti clockwise
up
moss
forest
Waitākere

Susan Glamuzina: Green

Summer Bat Walk Waitākere

Juliet Yates

The 'Summer Bat Walks' notice told me of an opportunity too good to miss. New Zealand bats are rare. I had never seen one, even though as a member of a Field Club I had spent nights in the bush, learning botanical names for plants and ferns, and many insects. There was never a sign of a bat.

Bats were the only land mammals in New Zealand before the introduction of predators like rats and stoats. Once there were three species, but only two survive. New Zealand has two kinds of bat: long- and short-tailed. The long-tailed bat has lately been found in several places near Auckland. The very rare short-tailed is an ancient species, unique to New Zealand. I had seen the display in the Auckland Museum and was fascinated by its habit. It feeds on the forest floor, unlike the long-tailed bat which flies from its roost and can swoop on its prey.

I signed up my family for the walk. The car was bursting with children and grandchildren. We parked at Cascade Kauri Falls Road carpark at 7.30pm and met the Ranger and the rest of the group.

There was a short walk to the viewing point. Below us was bush, and a stream. We sat on a slope and heard about conservation and then waited quietly, hoping for bats.

The Ranger explained that at dusk, long-tailed bats leave their roosts and some will search for insects near the stream. Bats are not blind, but at night their ears are more important than their eyes. As they fly, they make high pitched sounds and listen for echoes, to find and track prey, including insects. Bats use dynamic flight paths and sonar patterns to target and capture multiple prey items, showing they are not just swooping randomly, but are making calculations and planning their flight. After feeding, they return to their roosts to sleep out the rest of the night and day, hanging upside down.

New Zealand's second species is the short-tailed bat. It is an ancient species, unique to New Zealand. Its only Auckland location is Little Barrier. Unlike the long-tailed bat, it spends most of its time on the forest floor, and runs around, with folded wings, using its forearms and walking on its elbows. It feeds on insects, nectar, fruit and pollen. It can pollinate Rātā, Pōhutukawa and the Wood Rose (*dactylanthus*), a rare parasitic plant.

Suddenly the Ranger called '*Bat!*' Something very small with black, black wings swooped over the stream and circled up high, followed by two more. Not a whole swarm of bats, but exciting. This was the real thing. The long-tailed bat is found in Auckland, Waitākere and Hunua, Great Barrier, Little Barrier, and other places. Pākiri, Makarau, Kaukapakapa, Wainui. Clevedon, Riverhead, Swanson. Yet I had visited those areas many times and had never spotted a bat, until now.

Susan Glamuzina: Bat

Who Am I?

Kim Adams

Curling and turning strong in the forest, native and brown.

Firm in my place, nestled with the ferns, feeling tight and ready to burst, not to be touched but to be admired and sacred, to the earth, growing always, unique and special although I am one of many.

I am beauty and distinguished, but I am not proud, you see me but do I see you.

I'm in my realm for all to see, come closer but take nothing from me.

I'm exposed for all to see, I see you but do you see me.

I am strong, and nestled for all to see, let me be you and you be me.

Susan Glamuzina: Fern

Anniversary

Anni Docking

North Piha, at the spot where the road runs out, a track begins.

Ditch the car, don your wellies, and sally forth. Climb through the timber posts, hitch your pack higher and fasten the straps, then set off on your hike. Did you remember to pack the thermos? A champagne glass? Your journal? Hold the bouquet upright, let the white silk ribbons flow loose in the breeze. Follow the stream which sings over your left shoulder. Wind your way up the track taking care to avoid the muddied patches and stray sharp twigs. Reach the rough-treaded footbridge. Step across, avoid splinters which you know are waiting to strike, and veer left until you step into that moon- shaped glade. Notice how the tumbling stream curves oblique shapes into the hardest of rocks. Imagine a tangled family of eels who shelter in crevices beneath sandstone banks. Stand quietly for a moment - eyes closed - and listen out for the song of tūī overhead, the chatter of leaves. Spot flittering fantail wings; watch five pīwakawaka play as they dart from sunlight to shade. A distant waterfall echoes from over the next ridge.

Splashing sounds crackle through the January airwaves which are swarming with damp heat. Pungent scents of kauri, rimu, tī kōuka and mānuka rise from tangled undergrowth. Harakeke thrust spears toward the sun, korari daring to blossom so late in the season.

A sacred spot. Invisible spirits surround you. Recall that day slowly. Piece together the jigsaw, exploring forgotten edges, smoothing shapes into a familiar narrative frame. Two pre-school girls with gypsophila woven through blonde tresses, each wearing a white broderie anglaise petticoat dress. Bare toes peep from beneath flounced hems. Sweet sisters clasp fingers together in solidarity, eyes wide with an elusive combination of anticipation blending with trepidation. They are princesses today. You hug Gran, nod to Gran'pa who's chatting with Aunty beside the marquee. Glance at strangers nearby, share smiles. Await the formalities. Beneath this trunk belonging to the tallest tree leaning to the edge of riverbank, here where roots gnarled with time have been exposed to weather and tide; this place brims with memories which gather and swell into life.

Vows and rings are exchanged, kisses bestowed and received, guitars strummed, speeches given, futures bequeathed. Voices fall then rise, glasses clink, and guests mingle alongside a forest bride swathed in green silk organza. She glides like a swan through the crowd, greeting her guests. Groom snaps pictures. Later, in a darkroom below the holiday cottage, he will develop black & white photographs with crisp edges, sharp silhouettes. Right now, champagne bubbles tickle your tongue and chase each other into a parched throat. Swallow. You watch children tangle and giggle as they play ring-a- rosie and scatter petals upon lush grass still damp from morning's kiss.

Stop your meanderings. Drop your offering of flowers onto a shelf of rock beside the stream, to appease the forest gods.

Sit on a nearby tree trunk hollowed with rot, ragged bark dressed in multicoloured mosses and lichen.

Drift. Dream. Allow time to pass by unnoticed. Remember how water cascaded over steep rocks under moonlight that night, a few winters ago. Scrambling banks gave up their fight to cling to their earth and finally caved in, flooding the riverbeds until the valley floor became strewn with clumps of dirt. Eventually the entire glade plunged into the chasm and washed downstream.

Dusk is arriving with a quiver of rainbow and a splash of peach sky. You recall similar colours on your first trip, that Sunday adventure in the mid '80s. A pillion passenger on a motorbike descending to the south beach. You go roaring down the switchback-riddled road, wind slipping beneath the too-large helmet, arms gripping your boyfriend's waist tightly. You dismount, grateful to be alive, wobbling with remnants of fear. Your face is bleached ghostly white after a near-collision with a truck which dared to cross your centreline uphill on the worst of many hairpin bends. Roll your bike into the asphalt parking space, settle the red Honda onto its haunches. Eager to swim, you change into togs and begin to stroll to the sea. But the fine black sand is too scorching to bear casual walking, so you skip to the water's edge at speed while he laughs aloud at your antics. Later, you hold hands walking across moonlit dunes into seawater still hot at midnight. Months afterwards, his bike is sold the same week as the engagement ring is purchased. By the time mortgages are signed and babies arrive, freedom riding is forgotten. Laughter fades into the corporate jungle. You grow together like a kauri forest; robust roots give birth to strong-limbed branches. You love hard, but you have no time to swim. You forget how to fly.

Lift hand, swipe tears, then turn to the western sun which is wafting low upon the Tasman Sea. Stretch with the shadows as they merge into gloom.Hitch your pack and retreat into the bush line. Descend the trail toward the road, and rummage for the car keys lost deep in your pocket. Drive home.

Tonight, glance at the photograph framed upon the hallway wall as you pass by on the way to bed. Two sisters. Identical white dresses. The image is blurred with a patina of age, soft outlines tinged with sepia, edges slightly yellowed. Your baby girls are grown, yet still their huge eyes stare right into your history, telling whimsical truths about an era when the woodland faeries roamed about on the ridges of western hills filled with cascading waters. Bid the stars 'goodnight' and let your river of memories surf until the moon rises.

Dreams will chase all sorrows downstream to where the ocean awaits.

Tomorrow will come, faithfully as it always does. Wait for me there at our spot, where frothing tideline meets rivers of iron sand flowing beneath a bright watermelon sky.

Sweet dreams, my darling.

Dreams from Titirangi

Angela Reading

Storm in a Teacup

Rosie Lee

A high-pitched scream shattered the tranquillity of the bush.

I'd been enjoying the last three minutes of silence. It was the first quiet time I'd had since Nan got sick. I wanted to ignore it, but the scream sounded again, accompanied by a huge splash.

A stream of curses echoed through the moss-covered trees and ponga. Although the scream had made me think a woman was in trouble, the curses were definitely masculine.

I cautiously left the trail, taking note of the trees so I could find my way back. Following the noises, I arrived at the edge of the pool below the cascade. A blond-haired man around my age was splashing around in the middle of the water.

'I got it!' he exclaimed in a strong Australian accent, waving his phone at me. I caught a glimpse of a black and white bird displayed on it.

I gave him a disbelieving glance. 'You have got to be kidding me,' I muttered. 'That's a miromiro, a tom tit. They're common here. Maybe I should just leave you in that pool?' His well-developed abs, plainly visible through his wet t-shirt, didn't hurt the eyes, but I wondered how he'd got himself into the pool.

'Can you swim over here?' I asked him.

He lowered his phone and gave the water a sweep with the other arm, but stopped moving hastily. 'My leg is hurt.'

Hell. 'OK, I'll see if I can reach you.' I glanced around the area. Looked like I'd have to break a branch off one of the trees. Everything on the ground was rotten, just what you'd expect in a high rainfall area like the Waitāk ere Ranges. I found a branch dangling, half attached to the tree and heaved it off. 'Here, grab hold.' I thrust the branch towards him. He grabbed it all right, but when I tried pulling him to shore, his weight yanked me into the water.

'Archrch!' I should have just ignored him. To say it was icy would be an understatement, it felt more like something Captain Scott would have been used to in Antarctica.

I let fly a few words my Nan would have blushed to hear. The current caught me, swirling me closer to the guy. I reached out a hand and he grabbed it with his free one, still keeping his phone in the air.

Seriously? The stream washed us both out of the pool and into a rocky stretch of water.

'Forget your phone, we need to get out!' My water-filled backpack was threatening to drag me under, too. The side of the stream I'd come from was slick and steep. "Keep your head out of the water," I told him.

'No kidding,' he gasped.

My feet struck the bottom and I scrambled for the shallower edge. I managed to heave myself out on the wild side of the river, dragging the jerk with me.

'Thanks, this phone was expensive,' he panted.

'You're kidding me.' I couldn't believe his first thought was his stupid phone. He dragged himself further out of the water and started prodding his leg. There was a dribble of blood on his ankle. Perhaps he'd been bitten by an eel. I knew they liked to lurk in pools.

Still, it didn't look like he was dying, so I opened my backpack and retrieved the waterproof bag which held my snacks and emergency supplies before tipping the water out of the backpack.

I could do with a warm drink after that icy dunking. Good thing Nan always made me pack a thermos as well as a water bottle.

'Is that food? I'm starving,' the guy said.

I glared at him. 'Didn't you pack your own food? What were you thinking, going into the bush without anything?'

'My gear was at the top of the falls,' he admitted. 'I needed a photo to win a photo competition. And the cutest tit I ever saw was flitting around the top. It kept on hopping a bit further.' He stopped rubbing his leg and checked his phone again. 'This one's a winner for sure,' he said. 'Look, double tits!'

I didn't think I wanted to see what was on his phone, but the photo he showed me was a great image of a pair of tomtits, beak to beak.

'It's good, but was it worth landing us both here?' I dug out my peanut butter sandwiches.

'Why would you eat that junk?' he said, distracted. 'Don't you know about the rat hairs being in peanut butter?'

I looked at him in horror. "No way is that true. I guess you believe the one about there being a bit of cockroach in every bar of chocolate, too?"

'Don't tell me that!" He raised his hand in a stop gesture. "I love chocolate! It's even in my name, Theo. You know, like *Theobroma cacao*. The Latin name for chocolate.'

I shook my head at his gullibility, and his crazy name. 'Come on, smart-arse, eat a peanut butter sandwich and I'll give you some chocolate to follow.

Unless you're allergic?'

'Nah, it's all good. I'll eat it.' He held out his hand and I placed half of my sandwich in it.

Theo took a bite and chewed cautiously. 'I can taste rat,' he announced after swallowing.

'Well, then you can eat rat or starve.' I finished my own half - it tasted as delicious as always - and looked hungrily at the remains of his. I hadn't packed snacks for two.

Theo peeled apart the sandwich, checked its contents, then closed it again and shoved the rest in his mouth.

'I'm Pāua, by the way. Like the shellfish.' I got out my thermos and poured myself a cup of steaming black tea, jiggling the teabag with its tag. 'Want some?' Bet he's as cold as me.

'You're on! Let's get this par-tea started,' he joked.

I smiled. Maybe he wasn't such an idiot. I did like a good pun. 'I'm more into tranquili-tea.'

'You're a bit of a cu-tea.' He raised his eyebrows.

'I prefer hones-tea,' I suggested, lifting the cup to my lips. 'You obviously like living on the edge.' When I was done, I swished it out and poured him a cup.

'Guil-tea as charged,' he said, draining his cup. 'I often get caught in hot water.'

'If that had been hot water, I wouldn't be so cold now.' I pulled out my emergency blanket.

'Want to steep together?' he asked.

I snorted with laughter. "With a line like that, how could I say no?"

I wrapped the crinkly plastic blanket around us. It made sense to get warm together, after all.

I woke up some time later with raindrops on my face. Not only had the sun gone behind the clouds, it had set. My back was unexpectedly warm, and an unfamiliar weight draped over my body. I blinked more raindrops away. Where was his hand? My startle of surprise must have woken Theo, because his hand squeezed me reflexively, then retreated. I was colder without it.

I turned to Theo and his eyes opened sleepily. He gave a sudden jerk away from me.

'Spider!' he gasped.

I flicked hastily at my hair. An innocent wētā landed on the ground in front of me. 'Don't worry about that, it's a harmless cricket,' I told him. 'Anyway, our spiders aren't poisonous like yours are.'

He still got hastily to his feet, and cursed again when he put weight on his right leg.

'I might need a bit of help getting out of here.' He looked apologetic.

The rain increased. 'And we'd better get away from this stream,' I agreed. 'It'll flood.'

I packed away my things, pulling on my raincoat. 'Let's get going.' I slipped an arm around his waist. It felt unexpectedly cosy - at least it did until the first step when he stumbled and I discovered how much he weighed. Still, we made it up the first hill, and the second, before it got too dark, and way too slippery.

'We're going to have to do an overnighter, or we'll get lost, go over a cliff or something,' I said. 'Did they teach you how to make a bivouac in Oz?'

'I had a bivvy bag for that. With my gear.' He waved back towards the crashing water.

'Oh. Well, we can make do with ponga.' I demonstrated, stacking old fern fronds against a handy tree.

'You're sure about the spiders being harmless?' Theo asked. 'Only I can see littlered eyes in that tree.' He had his phone torch on and was looking suspiciously at the kānuka tree I was using as a bivvy base.

'I'm sure,' I said. 'Relax, and help me add more fronds if you want to stay dry.'

Before long we had a reasonable shelter. Theo even made a floor of kānuka leaves after I showed him how soft they were. We climbed into the small opening and I took off my raincoat, laying it over the leaves so we had something dry to sit on.

We sat in the dark, listening to the rain, and Theo tentatively reached over and touched my shoulder. 'I'm lucky you were there to rescue me,' he said. 'After all, it's not every day a bloke gets to see so many great tits in one day.'

The shelter wasn't enough to keep us warm. Even with our bodies close together, we shivered. After ten million or so raindrops had fallen, Theo started to take his pants off.

'I'm hot.'

Oh no, has he got hypothermia? I put my arms around him to hold his top on. Lightning flashed, penetrating the walls of our bivvy. The thunder that followed went on way too long.

'That's not thunder,' I realised as the sound changed pitch. 'It's a truck!' Sure enough the lights swung around. Unbelievable. We'd been metres from the road all along. Just like Captain Scott, so close to our objective without realising it.

Half an hour later, an ambulance drove away with my tea-loving, spider-hating Aussie. I felt surprisingly alone as I trudged back to my car.

It was only when I unpacked back the next morning that I found his phone number, scrawled on the tag of the teabag we'd shared.

Melissa Gunn: Predator or prey? A Toutouwai/North Island robin

Youth Section

Pies and Puns

Scarlet Q

As I watch the sunrise
I eat my pies
Looking at the sky
I think about the sun
and come up with puns

Campfire Joys

Rosie Shuttleworth

Birds chirp and children laugh

The moonlight fire crackles as gooey marshmallows are roasted

Branches and twigs snap under the sprinting feet of explorers

Owls hoot and adults gossip

The stars sparkle and the moon grins as the kiwi emerge from their burrows

Colour Sky

Jessica Barr

sunset: The sun drips low, a fiery glow paints the sky in hues that flow. Golden light fades into night whispers in peace fading sight.

sunrise: The sun ascends with soft warm rays touching caves where shadows play. Light spills in a gentle stream awakening the world.

Formation

Tilly Shuttleworth

Hope

Zoey Bayliss-Lane

Hope shines through the damp dark rock, gleaming in the gloom

It stands in its own spotlight, drawing all eyes to the cheerfulness after everything had been lost

A hole of happiness

Silhouette

Elsie Beachman

Black, green, and even blue.

So many different colours you appear to be.

A line of sentries – protecting the bay from the world beyond.

Your silhouette painted into the sky.

Such a beautiful sight.

The Guardian of Waitākere Forest

Savini Herath

Aroha, Tama, and Lila, young members of Waitākere Guardians were exploring the forest when they noticed the wai, stream, had turned murky and smelled of oil. Following the stream, they found leaking barrels near the old campsite.

Thinking fast, they built a barrier using branches and moss to stop the oil from spreading and rescued a few struggling freshwater eels. After calling the Department of Conservation, professional rangers arrived to clean up the spill.

Thanks to the Guardians' quick action, the forest and stream were saved and nature could thrive once again.

Falling

Keira Bailie

I tear through the dense bush with the enormous kauri towering over me. The thick odour of dirt wafted up my nose. I take a sharp turn and find myself at a waterfall. In awe of its extensive beauty. But then something shoves me, a hand. Suddenly I'm falling. The freezing water consumes me, and my lungs are screaming as I choke on the water. I am being dragged down by an unknown force and the salt water is penetrating my eyes making everything turning black. I give up and accept my fate and my lifeless corpse floats above the water. I am gone.

Sunset

Amelia Barr

I race to the beach
The pebbles of the road sharp against my heels
I can't miss it
The waves crash like my feet to the sand
My camera dangles from my neck
I stop, the shutter clicks
I sigh as the sun floats below the horizon
Oh, how the sunsets here are beautiful

A New Day

Sophie Sewell

Crunch goes the crispy apple
while the sun for sleepily
over my head.
My eyelids
fight to stay open
as the
sand around me begins to warm.
Flapping wings
soar above my head
and their high-pitched voices squawk.
Today will be
a new day!

Starlight Talks

Elsie Beachman

Gin shifted on the bench, breathing in the cool night air as she looked up at the sky. The dark silhouette of the Waitākere Ranges was set against the horizon framing the sea of stars shimmering in the sky, and the shadowy outline of the new moon.

A small smile graced her lips. You can see the stars so clearly out here. Away from the bright lights and hustle and bustle of the city behind the mountains. Soft footsteps rang out in the quiet of the night. Gin looked up, seeing Mae walking towards her, her boots padding across the grass.

"Heya," she said, mindful of the hour. Most people were getting ready for bed, getting into their pyjamas, and brushing their teeth.

"Hi," the red-haired woman said in acknowledgement, walking over and sitting down beside her. They sat in silence for a few moments, taking in the still, quiet night.

"What are you sitting out here for?" she asked.

Gin paused for a moment. "Just sitting," she said, "looking at the stars."

"Same here." Despite only being twelve, those still, quiet moments had stuck with her.

"I really like looking at the constellations," Gin remarked. "The Southern Cross is one of my favourites."

Mae shifted, leaning backwards towards the Milky Way. "Mine's Orion's Belt." She shifted her gaze back to Gin. "Do you know how to find south?" she asked.

"I think so. I find the Southern Cross, then find this bright star over there," Gin said, gesturing as she did, even though they wouldn't mean much from Mae's angle. "Then I find the point between them and take it down to the horizon," she said as she brought her hand together.

"I haven't heard of that way before," commented Mae.

"Well, I learnt it pretty briefly, so I could've forgotten or screwed up a step." "Why don't you show me what direction you think south is in. Then we can check if you got it right."

Gin swung her arm in the general direction towards the hills they had driven through on the way to camp. She pointed with her whole hand, a little habit she'd developed. First, she pointed with one finger, then two, and eventually decided to go for the whole shebang.

"Yup, that's south. Good work," Mae said, nodding her head towards where Gin had gestured.

"Sweet," Gin said, grinning and they fell back into comfortable silence.

"I'm going to go to bed now," said Mae. "Actually, we should both be

heading to bed now."

"Okay, okay," Gin said, getting up, taking one last look at the sky as she did. It had been a good night.

Pīwakawaka

Lucas Glamuzina

Canvas

Elsie Beachman

The salt spray of the sea

The shift of the sand

A canvas being replaced every few seconds

Rolling hills in cliffs

A silhouette against the sky

A frame displaying a painting

Waves approaching and retreating from the shore

Moving in unpredictable ways

Foam a constant form of beauty

A watercolour sky

Colours blending and bleeding into one another

The air alive with light

A flame flickering on the horizon

Bright and short

Basking the world in its golden glow

The canvas, the art

The frame and the tone

Glimmering in my mind's eye

An image of my own

Waitākere

Maryam Knowles

The shadow on the horizon

Always there comforting me, a shadow.

Something that's meant to be scary, comforting me.

How time changes perspective. It's the place with high canopies, with thousands of trees, plants, and birds.

It's the place where the fresh air and birdsong connects me to whenua, myself, and everyone who came before me.

Each step I am more at peace. If I'm feeling down, I know Waitākere will cheer me up.

I grew up in other countries. When I first moved I had never felt more alone. But it was that shadow, that found me. It made this home.

A Ting Adventure

Alexa Brown

Kauri trees spanning high above me. It takes me a second to realise that they are higher than they would normally be. I turn slowly on my heel, realisation settling in. Olive had noticed, towering above me, tongue lolling out of her mouth. 'Run', my brain screamed, it taking a second for the message to get through to my legs.

I tear through the undergrowth, leaf litter flying up around me. It barely registers with me that Olive has taken chase, adrenaline pumping through my veins. 'I need to get out of here, out of Olive's reach', is all I can think, jumping over a tree root. That's when it hits me. I should climb a tree. I glance around, trying to figure out my next move.

Just ahead of me I spot a kauri tree, it's bark ridged and wrinkled, perfect for climbing. Knowing that this will likely be my only chance, I speed up, jumping onto the tree. I quickly hoist myself higher and higher, for what feels like an eternity. I brave a look down, Olive barking excitedly up at me from the base of the tree. My arms are aching, but the lowest branches are just above my head, almost in my reach. I go slower, the adrenaline starting to wear off, my heart slowing in my chest. I pull myself up onto a branch, and I feel I can finally relax.

Kōkako

Élise Cater

Kōkako
A feathery ghost
Song echoing through trees
Scurrying over branches
Gone
And yet
A glimpse of grey
It's back!
A wonder returning
From uncertain death
Joyous calls are heard
As they see it again
Aotearoa's ghost
Kōkako

Élise Cater: Kōkako

Footprints

Lucas Glamuzina

Clouds leaving a footprint

Slowly moving along the rich landscape

Causing a subtle sense on movement and change over the otherwise unmoving landscape

A placid smell mixing with a wet earthy one leans into the cloudprint feelings

The trees unmoving regime will be here for years to come

These things will last long after our times

The solemn watching clouds forever

Flows

Frankie Glamuzina

The river flows as the sky blows down on the trees, the trees start singing with birds and the birds fly over the seas towards the bees 🐝

End of Youth Section

Ocean's Mystery

Cathryn Davy

I peep into the ocean's world
dark walls around me
incoming marshmallow waves
crashing on the hermit's home
embracing change
keep crawling on
What's that blue shimmer?
shimmering the sky up high
shimmering on the ground too!
a reflection of that sparse world!
it makes us wonder, think and learn.
The ocean is so humbling

Species Imaginaries

Lucy Boermann

in walking exhibition drive (eastward) and the sleeping slug.

what is in a name? I see a half-buried pipe, no, a sleeping-slug gurgling its way through bush and track, runners pass by.

what does the environment offer us, the individual, and what does the individual offer the environment?

James Gibson defines affordances of the environment as what it offers the animal, what it provides or furnishes, either for good or ill.

what if we were to design from the premise that we are wrong? what if we were to extend Gibson's definition of affordance as a singular "one-way" event-happening to that of an intentional "return-event" – a reciprocation through collective making (ie a responsive learning-event in situ)?

I wonder how the sleeping slug might intervene...

Glengarry Road

Barbara Peterson

I remember how we'd sit in the sun on your deck

You, strumming your guitar and singing

Me, bathing in the fierce autumn warmth

Before the day's light vanished behind the trees.

We went out for dinner, you and I

On Valentine's last year

You told me you loved my poetry

You made one of my poems into a song.

In winter you'd switch on the heat pump if I was cold

Even if embers still glowed in the fireplace

You'd fill up the bathtub and give me your trackpants

I'd trace your lower back with icy hands.

Even when you left, you stayed. And stayed

Strummed and sang, laughed at my jokes

Made me lunch and dinner and, and

Held on as you let go, lingering, fingertips still touching

As you stretched like a shadow into the night

Susan Glamuzina: Nightfall

Back yard   Back story

Alexandra Fraser

The back yard was silent for months
no distraction from our frame of mind
only the creak of the garden swing

But today suddenly there is bird song
(a neighbour must have set rat traps)
 cackle and whistle shrill and trill

Dove and pigeon synchronise bleats
the tūī croaks and gargles
the blackbird sings joy

A ginger cat pauses in his perambulations
sits meditatively centre lawn
stares at the same spot for half an hour

He ignores the ducks the ducks ignore him
instead they scramble up to our deck
looking for last night's dinner debris

if only someone could set anxiety traps
 (would they be baited with chocolate
hot buttered toast?)

With anxieties tempted and slayed
we would once again be singing into
the flurry of wind in our surrounding trees

Susan Glamuzina: Natural knots

Between the Tide and the Sea

Kerry Clark

Auckland's west coast is a dramatic landscape of scorching black-sand beaches against a backdrop of lush, temperate rainforest painted fifty shades of green, called the Waitākere Ranges. Sunday, 16th November 2003 added searing blue sky to the palette.

Smart phones hadn't been invented yet. My radio clock woke me up with the news. Twelve sperm whales had stranded on Karekare Beach. Volunteers were pouring in. We had a 40-minute drive from our home in Titirangi, and every minute counted if the whales were to stay alive until the high tide could take them out to sea again. If we were to help, we had no time to lose.

The children, a ten-year-old and eight-year-old, grabbed buckets large and small, as I rummaged for old drop sheets and worn-out tea towels. With the imagination of the young, their eyes had filled with tears at the mental picture they formed of the disaster, and desperately hoped to save some whales. The beach car park was packed to the gunnels, so we parked on a tussocky verge and joined the crowd of volunteers on the sandy track. At the beach, Department of Conservation workers were directing operations. People with clipboards and walkie-talkies were everywhere. The beach was now a series of black mountains, each surrounded by people with buckets and sombre faces. The gleaming black sand, decorated with foamy patterns, had streaks of red running down to the water line. That was a shock. We were utterly still for a moment, then both children started to cry. One of the majestic mammals had already been euthanized and we spotted an official carrying a gun. I explained the concept of *killing-for-kindness*, but realized we were sorely unprepared for such a raw life-and-death lesson. Did they want to go home? No, they were both determined to help, so we filled our buckets from the waves and took them to the nearest whale. She was lying on her side, a whopping 15-20 metres long. Maybe the size of a bus. One giant flipper was moving slightly and the one eye we could see was open, aware. You could see her pain. She looked at us, our eyes actually connected as though she were asking us, *specifically us*, for help. We splashed and filled and splashed and filled. We draped sheets over her and soaked her with water.

A shot sounded and we froze again then redoubled our efforts. The children were getting very tired, tears running down their faces but would not give up. A DoC worker came over to us. "I'm afraid she's dead." We looked, and sure enough, the whale's bright, intelligent eye was cloudy white now, and her flipper was still. We looked around. Not one of the mountains had been moved at all, despite diggers creating channels, and hundreds of people carefully excavating around them. I noticed strange lumps of what looked like hardened scrambled eggs, shot with waxy gold like kauri gum, littering the beach. A few volunteers were gathering the lumps. I asked what it was and it turned out to be ambergris, excreted from the intestine of sperm whales. (I had heard about ambergris; used for centuries in perfume manufacturing). But most perfumiers now have synthetic fixatives, surely no need for sperm whale ambergris any more; so I wondered why people were collecting it.

Perhaps for souvenir value?

Perhaps to sell. It is called floating gold and is purportedly worth its weight in gold.

Was there a black market in ambergris?

My mind was all over the place- any place other than dwelling on the mysterious self-destruction of these incredible creatures.

As we left the beach, officials had already cordoned the area off and set guards for the night. The late-arriving 'ambulance-chasers' wereturned away. Iwi had been notified.

Next morning the news announced that all the remaining whales had been shot.

I had to explain to the children that these strandings were not yet understood by scientists, but we know now that, once rescue becomes impossible, euthanasia is the only kind option.

It was a very doleful, subdued drive to school for all of us.

Susan Glamuzina: Bluebottle stranding

Waitākere Ranges, Te Wao Nui-a Tiriwa

Suzanne Gee

waking slow cool mist Karekare Valley
riroriro - grey warbler, your long trill, inside my head
low thrum jet engine 747 overhead
tick tock battery clock
are you on daylight saving time?
gidday! I'm on Waitākere Ranges time
lonely sigh solitary rustle
onion peel inside a paper bag
do you seek my company?
clinging to tānekaha
tenacious cicadas contracting tymbals
compete zzzz zzzz with my tinnitus
pink gin squeeze of sour lemon
toast to the West Coast sunset
lavender light hovers
kererū kererū
ko wai kōrua?
he ātaahua kōrua

Waitākere – Lost and Found.

Caroline Carlyle

You are an enigma.
From haunted hills,
hiding unresolved sins,
to strong dark waters stealing sand from your flat shores.

You are a thief.
Taking life from lungs,
and children from whanau,
leaving only holes in hearts and stones in their souls.

You are ghostly.
Holding supernatural legends.
Battles in the sweet swirling mists
between the patupaiarehe and tūrehu (faerie folk).

You are depression.
Bringing squatters,
diggers of gum, and
hidden stashes amongst the honest leaves.

You are beautiful.
Sprinkling waterfalls with fairy dust,
showering lush scrub that
covet streams, and end at mighty Kauri.

Morning in the Waitākere Ranges

Edna Heled

Mōrena
Faint light
Piping at me
Through the window
Should I go or should I stay
In this midwinter sunny new day
Outdoor is calling like the Pied Piper of Hamelin
So is the warm blanket that does not let its guard down
Still carrying the fragrances of my chocolate covered dreams
Giving me permission to sink in, a soloist in my undercover concert
Listening to dissolving fragments of worlds that wake at night
Music to my ears which my ears alone can hear and long
I will not be sharing this with the outside world
Lazy angels of a new day, indecisive like me
Bless me anyway, say it will be alright
Find me a way to get out of bed
To forests to bushes to birds
Something big is about
To happen
Today

Hike

Akenese Faletagoai

Race Day

Carl Kjellberg

Her name was Jane—not Calamity Jane, though her friends often joked she was a calamity in the kitchen. She was the fastest gun in the west. West Auckland, that is. The dastardly possum gang, notorious for nibbling every ripe fruit on her apple tree, learned to fear her. She could shoot the ears off a possum at a hundred yards with her BB gun.

And my name is Mr Snuffles. If you saw a photo of me, like the one Jane keeps on the mantel piece beside her BB gun, you would agree that I am a rather fine-looking young gelding. You would also likely agree that Mr Snuffles is not at all a good name for such a handsome beast. A name like Lightning Bolt, Angels Delight or, maybe at a stretch, Trigger would be much more appropriate. But Mr. Snuffles it is. I guess she must have been having one of her calamity moments the day she named me.

Living on the west coast has its perks. I have my own paddock with plenty of grass, but best of all, there's a beach nearby. I love it when Jane takes me down to the beach to wade through the surf. There's nothing like it, especially on a hot summer afternoon. One morning, as Jane was riding me down the beach, a middle-aged woman approached us.

"Hi, my name is Caroline," she said with a big smile. "Would you be interested in entering your horse in the Karekare beach race?"

"When is it?" Jane asked.

"Saturday, the 18th of April," Caroline said, handing Jane a flyer. "Oh, and by the way, it's going to be a fancy-dress event."

Great, I thought. I can just see it now: Jane, sitting on my back wearing her gardening hat, her BB gun slung over her shoulder, and everyone laughing at us. I am really looking forward to that. Not!

When race day came around, Jane entered my paddock wearing a long, flowing dress. Her hair was lightly curled, she had long, pointed ears, and she wore a delicate band of gold upon her head. For a moment, I didn't recognise her. She looked gorgeous! To top it all off, she put a bridle on me that was decorated with what looked like diamonds and led me down to the beach, where we were met by a man holding a clipboard.

"Name?" he asked.

"Lady Galadriel, High Elf of Lothlórien. And this is Shadowfax, lord over all horses who live on Middle-earth," Jane replied.

I felt a warm feeling surge through my body, and in that moment, everything seemed to change. The man gave Jane a wry smile and handed her his clip-board and a pen. As I lined up at the starting line with Jane upon my back, I felt somehow bigger and stronger. When the starting gun went off, I surged past all the other horses and won by a country mile. Jane was given a gold medal, even though I had done all the hard work. But I didn't care. I was Shadowfax, lord of all horses, and she was my lady, even if it was for only for a little while.

Piha Vibes

Jordan Hanna

The sounds of waves crashing
      fill my ears bringing a
         calming sensation to me
The suns orange tinge
      fills the sky as it gets ready
        to rest for the night
Birds chirping
      around me as they soar
        through the sky
Sand below my feet
      I walk along the beach
        peaceful in my mind

Susan Glamuzina: Sunset

Laingholm

Susan Glamuzina

This is the first time I've taken that road, the road that will become my normal. In time I will know the people that live here, wave at them, I will celebrate milestones with them, and mourn with them as they grieve. We will walk our dogs together and push our children on the swings. This road is my future, right here. Right now is the only time I will ever drive down it for the very first time.

I pull into the driveway, walk in my own front door – first time, and the movers have done their part. The furniture is in the lounge, set up in the wrong direction. Facing the TV, not the phenomenal view. I wanted to see the kauri and ferns. The bed was set up in the right room and even in the right place, side tables where they are meant to be and it only takes me an hour to hang my clothes, set up the side lamps, pull back the curtains and take in that view, my view of the Waitākere ranges down to the Manukau heads. Laingholm's finest view.

I put my hand on my tummy. He or she will grow up with this view. He or she will experience the very best that the nature has to offer. We will go counting snails, looking for wētā. We will go fairy hunting together, and at the bottom of the property, where it meets the Manukau harbour, we will go kayaking, but only when the tide is in because, when the tide's out those mudflaps are not kayak friendly.

Six months ago, I thought I knew my life. One random night with a random man I'd never see again, and then a family estate I hadn't counted on. I'd rather not have money that way, but it has given me the possibility to fund my changing life. I'd given up on motherhood in my 20s, motherhood hadn't given up on me. My job has easily changed to be remote. I don't think I'll miss city life - the constant hum of traffic and people.

I open the window. A fantail darts, a tūī makes its music. The bird life is all I can hear - no car tyres, no one brokering a deal on their phone, nothing but peace and quiet. I'm excited about me and my mini-me exploring the wilderness and living a life of calm. Once I have the house in order, I can plant our veggie garden, watch my food grow as my baby grows within me. I never thought I'd wanted motherhood, yet only three months to go. I can hardly wait. Each breath I get closer to holding him or her. Each moment I'm closer to becoming complete and having the life I never knew I wanted.

Susan Glamuzina: Nikau and fern grove

Gravestones

Laura Whitaker-Hill

Can you mourn a tree?
Silver, spectral giants of
The forest – dying.

Each foothold in soil
Laced with microscopic spores
Infecting the host.

Cones, leaves, bark starving
Kai for kākā, kōkako,
Kererū fading.

Roosts for ruru, gone
Taonga lost forever
Ngahere empty.

Can you mourn a tree?
Ancient, tall, masts in a sea
Of green. We grieve for you.

The Judsons and Nihotupu

Jenny Clay

There is a path next to the carpark off Piha Road, not far from Scenic Drive, that leads to the Upper Nihotupu Dam. It passes close to where William Frederick Judson had a cabin and a house in the Waitākere Ranges, before the area was developed for Auckland's water supply.

Fred married Emily Marian Edger, a music teacher, singer, and his first cousin in 1879. Their only child, Dora, was born within the year. When Fred began to buy land in the Waitākere Ranges in the late 1880s, he was living with Marian on their property in Ponsonby.

Marian came from a family of five siblings, four girls and a boy. Two years earlier her younger sister, Kate Edger, had become the first woman in the British Empire to graduate from a university with a Bachelor of Arts. The youngest, Lilian, followed Kate into academic success. Their father, Samuel, a non-denominational preacher, encouraged all his children in independent thinking.

Fred Judson would take the train to Waikumete station, by the new cemetery, and then walk or go by horse up the Waitākere Ranges to reach his land. He built a cabin in the area of the present Upper Nihotupu dam, and continued to purchase hundreds of acres. In 1891, he applied to the Waitematā County Council for a road to be defined to his property.

His nephew, Stanley Judson, came to live with him for four years, attending Oratia and Henderson schools.

Lilian Edger set up a private girls' school at the Ponsonby property, where Marian taught music, and Dora attended. In 1894 Marian took Dora to Europe to study at the Frankfurt Conservatorium in Germany. Lilian left New Zealand a few years later to spend most of her life in India involved in theosophy and teaching. The Ponsonby property sold to their sister, Eva, and her photographer husband, Charles Hemus.

Fred began to build a new house close to the road to Piha and near the Nihotupu Stream. In 1899 Annie and Thomas Elliman, or Eleman, built a large boarding house nearby. The Scenery Conservation Society advertised a trip in March 1900 to the area, which was regarded as picturesque in relation to the falls, the bush, and the stream. At the Nihotupu bridge they'd separate into those going to the nearest of the falls, and people who wanted to remain by the houses of Judson and Elliman, where Mrs Elliman would 'provide refreshments at a moderate charge.' [1]

Marian and Dora had returned from Europe, and Dora was teaching and giving concerts in Auckland. She wrote in April to Amy Causley, a family friend, who had attended Lilian's school. 'We had a second camping party' at Nihotupu 'after you went. ... ten of us' and 'went up by moonlight on Friday evening, ... over to the Coast next day and back'. At Easter 'if the weather keeps fine we are going to have a picnic'. The new Unitarian minister, Mr Jellie, was to accompany them 'as he has not been to the Ranges yet – Aunt Eva is coming too if she can' and her daughters, Geraldine and Irene. [2] Marian later wrote 'when we were up there at Easter we went through the Forest reserve down to the lower Fall, the big one', which was the Nihotupu Falls.[3]

By 1901 Marian joined her husband. In February she was making jam from blackberries their visitors had picked along West Coast Road. In May she said 'the roads are beginning to get bad; and there is no more going to the Falls for the present – but Dora and I went for a very pretty walk along the tramline towards Henderson on Sunday … it is lovely, all through the bush.'[4]

Irene Hemus wrote enthusiastically about a trip in October. 'Aunt Marian, Dora, Mr Jellie and I caught the evening train to Waikumete and walked up to the bush mansion', from Glen Eden. 'We had two showers on the way but didn't get wet, arrived there about half past nine rather tired and a little bit hungry'. In 'the morning the three of us just strolled around the bush on the hill opposite after clematis which Mr Jellie had never seen before and bought home some watercress that we found at the bottom of the hill. After dinner we wasted the afternoon up at the kauris.'[5]

Dora moved to Nelson to teach at the School of Music and at Nelson Girls' School. Marian wrote to Amy in February 1902 'We have been quite lively here this summer – there have been many staying at Mrs Eleman's and I have had a few visitors and am expecting some more now'.[6] In 1904 she wrote about their house, the 'verandah is nearly finished and it is a lovely one, eight feet wide, getting the sun nearly all day and sheltered from the cold winds, we shall enjoy it in the winter.'[7] By August she was planning to visit her sister, Kate Evans nee Edger in Wellington. Friends of the Judsons, Mr and Mrs Hartnell, were 'coming to stay with Mr Judson while I am away, so we shall get a little more done to the building'.[8] At the end of 1905 Marian joined her sister Lilian in India for four years.

One of the things the Waitākere Ranges is known for is rainfall. This made the Auckland Council decide to establish water catchments in the area, when they were looking for a new water supply for the growing city. There had been discussions since 1900. A wooden Nihotupu dam was constructed in 1902, and an early pipeline to Titirangi. The Council wished to acquire more land for the Waitākere and the Nihotupu watersheds. A proposed site for a storage reservoir was not far from Judson's place, with an enormous natural basin. The mayor, Arthur Myers, and Auckland councillors visited in February 1906, and lunch was served near the Judson house. It was the only residence still occupied. The buildings of the Elliman's had already been sold and removed.

The house and hundreds of acres of Judson's and nearby land were taken for the Nihotupu dam and watershed, and the 'watershed Waitākere' under the 'The Auckland Waterworks Extension Act 1904'. Nihotupu, Huia and Waitākere streams were to be diverted or 'impounded'. [9]   The protections put in place for the water supply encouraged the regeneration of native bush.

Fred Judson's spirit did not appear to be discouraged by his loss. He'd bought a property from A.S. Nodder in 1903, and two years later had a boarding house built on the knoll on Scenic Drive, before the Piha turn-off. The Waiatarua boarding house opened in 1906 with thirty rooms and a large dining room. It had a view of the Waitematā harbour and Auckland city on one side, and the Manukau harbour on the other.

The name may have come from a Māori workman who helped to build it. He described Waiatarua as meaning the song of two waters. Other translations or interpretations are two waters singing or view of two waters. [10]

Fred had a cottage built along the road around 1915. Construction of the concrete Upper Nihotupu Dam started in the same year and was completed in 1923. The Waiatarua boarding house passed to Fred's nephew, Stanley Judson, and was managed by others.

Fred would still come and sit by the fireplace and read from the library of books. He was the first officer in charge of the telephone station at Nihotupu into his eighties. When he died in 1931, at the age of eighty-six, the cottage and adjacent land passed to his daughter Dora.

Dora was at the cottage with her cousin's daughter, Mickey, in May 1945 when she wrote, 'We were sorry to miss the announcement of the end of European hostilities. We have no radio but get the paper, sometimes rather late. It is a great relief to know at least the fighting in Europe has ceased.' She said, 'Mickey and I and two elderly lady friends came ... to our little hill cottage on the 29th of April and expect to stay ... ten days longer. We are still living in our home in Epsom but do come up here ... though not so often as before the war – it is awkward getting up and down and the problem of supplies is quite a big one as the store which used to be quite adequate is now not nearly as well stocked and only opens at bus times.

However we bring lots of stuff with us' and 'love coming here – the bush is so fresh and beautiful'.[11]

The boarding house became flats in the forties. It was converted into the Dutch Kiwi restaurant in 1960, which burned down ten years later. Dora moved to the cottage permanently, and when she died in 1966 left it to Mickey, who had married John Cooke. It was only demolished around 2017. The name Waiatarua remains, long since replacing Nihotupu, as the name of the bush suburb up West Coast Road at the top of the Waitākere Ranges.

1. New Zealand Herald, 24 March 1900.

2. MS1626 Amy Causley Papers, Auckland Museum. Dora Judson to Amy Causley, 8 April 1900.

3. MS1626 Ibid. Marian Judson to Amy Causley, 6 May 1900.

4. Ibid, 29 May 1901

5. MS1626 Ibid. Irene Hemus to Amy Causley, 6 October 1901

6. MS1626 Ibid. Marian Judson to Amy, 19 Feb 1902

7. Ibid, 26 March 1904

8. Ibid, 5 August 1904

9. New Zealand Herald, 28 April 1905

10. Song of Two Waters by Jeanne Wade, p. 4, 2nd edition 1997

11. MS1626 Amy Causley Papers, Auckland Museum. Dora Judson to Amy Hansen, 19 May 1945

Jenny Clay: Towards Upper Nihotupu Dam

Te Piha / Lion Rock

Deborah Leigh

Majestic taonga of old; Te Piha
a massive, volcanic, feline-shaped beast
who lies, sphinx-like, on guard
ever-watching the western seas
for Tangaroa's storms & invaders.
A monolithic tor of rock
rising up out of the seam
between black iron-sands & white roiling surf.
The latter brings excitement,
cleansing & deep joy,
but sometimes death.

Te Piha, cloaked in green;

a mantle of pōhutukawa, harakeke & grasses

that whip to & fro in the wildling winds.

Your little shallow nooks & ana

are sheltering places for gulls & their young

&, in times long gone, likely for fishing kete

or taonga or the tapu dead.

Ah, if only you, Te Piha could talk & tell us

your stories of yesteryear

when warriors ran up your flanks

in their muscular finery

to take their places as watchmen & defenders

in the invasions & wars of old.

The last of which, in 1825

when your people, Te Kawerau ā Maki

finally had to flee down to Karekare

where they eventually & tragically

lost their noble fight

against the invading Ngā Puhi

who sought utu from the Ngāti Whātua

with whom your people had an ill-fated alliance.

How the wāhine must've keened

over their near-obliterating losses

of almost all members of the their iwi

& all of their whenua.

Many years ago when I lived out Karekare

& was in mourning,

I liked to walk alone on the beach in the evenings

when the locals & the manuhiri had all left.

One time, when there was only Waka-dog & me to see,

we were blessed by the sudden emergence

of many cloaked Māori spirits

standing on the sands not far from us

all very still

silently looking out to sea.

A sight I'll never forget

& one I quietly withdrew from

not wishing to disturb their stately vigil.

For, not far from where they all stood

is the old spirit-path above the waves

upon which their dead fly

on their way to their final resting places

in the seas of the far north.

Haere, haere, haere rā.

Translation notes from Te Aka Māori Dictionary.co.nz:

Taonga / treasure

Tangaroa / Māori god of the sea & fish

Pōhutukawa / large native coastal tree

Harakeke / flax

Ana / cave

Kete / basket, kit

Tapu / sacred, prohibited, restricted, set apart, forbidden

Te Kawerau ā Maki / Māori tribe of Piha region

Karekare / neighbouring beach south of Piha

Ngā Puhi / Māori tribe of the northern region of Aotearoa, NZ

Utu / to repay, pay, respond, avenge, reply, answer

Ngāti Whātua / Māori tribe of the area from Kaipara to Auckland

Wāhine / female, women, feminine, ladies, wives, plural of wahine

Iwi / extended kinship group, tribe, nation, people, race

Whenua / land, country, nation, state, ground, territory, placenta

Manuhiri / visitor, guest

Haere rā / good-bye, farewell (said to someone leaving)

Little Muddy Creek

M Bulte

A reimagining of a true story

I spend much of my time looking out over the farm through a mist of grey these days. Little Muddy Creek, they call it, and not without cause.

Everything is such a far cry from Bruges, city of canals and high, narrow brick houses. The houses here are mere huts in comparison, thin wooden walls of local timber, too thin to keep out the cold. The trees and shrubs grow fast—and no wonder, the rain here is as pervasive as that of my homeland— and they're the wrong shade of green, muddy like the ground. The birds sound wrong and there are no squirrels or foxes. The only thing that is familiar is the mud and the rain. So very much rain. It will be my undoing, I fear.

The boys have a job working on the roads, which are always mired knee- high in winter. That is just as well, because most of the seeds cousin Antoine sent over went mouldy on the long sea journey.

Possibly he was right to be concerned about us making our way in this foreign land, but what else were we to do? I could not show my face in Bruges again after my brilliant invention turned out not to be quite as brilliant as I'd first thought. The council had put all that money into promoting my new tiles, but alas! The rain was my undoing there too.

Fortunately, Marie has found herself a good position with the P—family and sends money back to keep us in bread. She is as close as is possible to roads worthy of the name; there are even paved footpaths here and there in the centre of the city that is growing up around the harbour. But that is not the place for me; no, I shall keep my disgrace to myself here on the farm. There is no need for anyone here to know my shame, and were I to learn the language, as Marie suggests, and socialise overmuch, then surely my story would come out. That would be much to the detriment of my young family, so I will not do it.

Dear Marguerite stays with me; since my beloved wife passed away so suddenly, she is rather less spritely than usual, but at least she does not speak of becoming a governess like her sister, however much that would better her own situation. Instead, she looks after the chickens, churns the butter as her mother used to do, and takes an absurd amount of time talking to the small grey birds they call robins. Alas, they do not have the cheery red breasts of the robins in our homeland, but Marguerite does not mind. She does not remember those red-breasted birds, and seems happy here. That is a solace.

When they get back from their stint on the roads, the boys will move the cattle. They speak of moving altogether, of land to the south which is not so steep, now that the inheritance from their cousin has come through. But I? I shall not leave this land that claimed my beloved. I will stay, and paint, and listen to the strange calls of the birds, and watch the rain falling like tears over the farm and the water, and I will remember the days in Belgium when we were both young and healthy and full of hope for the future.

Such hopes we had. Lost in the rain and the mud.

Jenny Clay: Reflections

Into the Wild

Justine Newnham

It's a fine day to do that walk in the Waitākere Ranges Ava from work always talks about. She has become a good friend to me since I started my new job in a new country a few months ago. It was a coincidence that she comes from the same state as I come from, Nevada. She has been here in Auckland for over a year now and loves it. She especially likes the Waitākere Ranges.

'It's a great stress release,' Ava said after I mentioned how stressed I was lately. Maybe I'm a bit homesick. 'It's one of the best things about Auckland. Well, one of the many. I can't believe you haven't been there already. It's like, one minute you are driving in Suburban and the next you are in this amazing dense forest. And I mean dense. I have not seen anything like it back home in Nevada. You will be amazed,' Ava continued.

'Yeah, it is really lush here in Auckland,' I replied.

'I would walk the track across the road from the "Arataki Visitors Centre". I think it is called the "Arataki Nature Trail". An easy walk. It even has plant identification signs of some of the native plants. Which is cool. Will you be going by yourself?' Ava asked.

'Yes I prefer to go alone,' I replied.

'Just make sure you stick to the tracks. Don't want you to go missing or anything,' she advised.

'Yes of course I will stick to the tracks,' I replied, but don't really understand why she had to mention that.

Now, I am entering the track that Ava suggested. Spotted the plants with their identifications. I must be on the right track. There are a lot of shrubs and trees here that I have noticed planted around the city, but never have I seen so many densely packed together.

Instantly, I realise why Ava likes walking through the forest. It is unlike anything I have experienced back home in Nevada. I feel the calmness Ava mentioned. The air feels damp, but fresh. There are many birds making lots of sounds. They seem happier here too. I recognised the Tūī and a little bird with a fan-like tail that has come to greet me. It's nice to see such friendly birds.

As I walk further into the bush the intense light of day dims as the canopy takes over. Some of the sun's rays make it through the gaps in the canopy to appear like shooting stars. A musky smell lingers in the air as the temperature drops. Chilly, but refreshing. I became a bit concerned as I only brought a thin cardigan to wear. But I was not going back to the car now. I thought maybe if I walked a bit faster I would keep warm.

As I walked deeper into the bush the trees blocked out the traffic noises.

The birds kept singing and the cicadas produced their high pitch sound like nothing I've ever heard before. Suddenly I spotted an interesting mushroom. I am fascinated by mushrooms.

Never seen any back home. It's too dry. I just recently bought an amazing book for identifying New Zealand mushrooms. Desperately wanting to take a photo to identify them later using my book. But I will need to go off the track to get a closer look. It's only about five meters away from the track. It should be easy to get back on track again.

Upon arriving at the mushrooms I spotted a larger group of mushrooms just a couple more meters further into the bush. I had to take photos of them all. So many different varieties in just a small area. I could not believe how lucky I was to find them all together. Never seen anything like it. I tried to add some of the photos to Instagram for my friends back home to see. But was disappointed to realise I was out of the WIFI range. Will just have to send them later.

It was time to continue my walk through the bush. I stood up from the mushrooms and turned around. I could not see where the track was and couldn't remember what direction I came from. I tried walking in a direction that looked like where I came from, but I could not see any tracks. I tried another direction and failed again. It was as if the forest blocked all the tracks from my vision with its denseness. I could be trapped here forever? I thought. I really did not know what to do and started to panic.

I started to think does the bush not want me to go? Oh, that's silly talk, I thought. I need to think seriously now. What am I going to do? It really feels like I have lost my bearings. Not sure where North, South, East or West is? No internet or cell phone coverage. I feel so hopeless. Now I understand why Ava said to stay on the track. It's a bit late to worry about that now. Stuck with no warm clothing, hardly any food and only a mouthful of water left in my water bottle. How will I survive? My emotions started to rise to the surface, forcing tears to release. All I could think of was, that I am doomed. Life for me is over. Just imagining the news headlines "Another person dies in the Waitākere Ranges". I could become famous for all the wrong reasons.

There was no need to feel sorry for myself. I kept telling myself to pull it together. I should at least try to find the track. Walk around a bit. Maybe I could find cell phone coverage somewhere. I just walked anywhere that felt easy to walk as the bush is dense and the footing is uneven. Each step forward takes effort. Especially when encountering many low branches.

Eventually I felt too exhausted. I had enough and did not have the will or energy to move anymore. I came to the conclusion that I was really lost. Stuck. I do not know what to do. Too many thoughts raced through my head. I just need to slow down those thoughts and try to meditate for a moment. I want to calm my mind to think clearly about what to do next. All I could do was let fear override my thoughts. So I tried to listen to the birds. They calmed my thoughts. I didn't realise what beautiful songs they sang.

As the birds chirped loudly, I heard something in the distance that was strangely familiar. It was not a bird song. It was growing louder and louder. It sounded like humans. Suddenly I felt hope. These voices slowly moved closer and closer. Then reached their maximum volume point at only six meters away from where I stood. Then the sounds slowly faded away into the distance. I couldn't see them as the bush is so dense, but I have an idea where they were and that is where I aim to go. I felt a good feeling that I was going to make it. However, there was no way I could walk in a straight line to that point. There were too many trees and branches in the way. I just had to try my best not to veer off the line too much, as I worried

I may not find the track again. A few scratches appeared on my arms as I proceeded to push the branches aside. Not worried about the pain, as I was determined to find the track. That was the only thing on my mind. The energy I used to push through became unbearable. The trees were not letting me through with their densely packed branches that went on forever. I wished that I had called out for help when I first heard the voices. It seems so silly to do so as I couldn't see them. They would not see me either. Yet they seemed so close..

I continued until I became stuck behind a large branch with spiky leaves of a Totara. I could not see a way around it either. Suddenly, I caught a glimpse of the track. I had to choose either to climb over the branch. Too high and spiky. Or crawl on my belly under it. The crawl was the best option and although I felt fatigue I was determined not to give up. I am so close now. Using all the energy I had left I dragged my body through the small gap. Leaf litter found its way down my T-shirt. I kept imagining bugs in that leaf litter crawling all over my body. Eek. I just had to block those thoughts and keep going. The Totara's spiky leaves continued to scratch my face, and it caught a knot in my hair as if it was stuck in a fine tooth comb. This caused my head to become stuck. The rest of my body could not move either as it was wedged in between large branches. I felt so annoyed as I was nearly there. I could almost touch the track with my nose if only I could move my head just a little bit more.

'Help!' I gave up on my pride and shouted. All I need is someone to yank me out of this bush.

'Help!' I yelled again a bit louder.

Someone must have heard me as it sounded like a couple of people running in my direction. I yelled out for help again in case they couldn't see me

'Hello. How can we help you?' A lady came closer to my head.

'I am stuck. My hair is stuck in this tree. I can't move. All I need is for someone to pull myself out. Can you do that?' I asked, 'Can you reach in and grab my shoulders and pull me out?

'Yes. Yes, We can try,' the lady turned to her friend behind her. Then they bent down and reached into the spiky bush to grab a shoulder each.

'On the count of three. One, two, threeeeee.' The friend commanded. Slowly they dragged me out from the bush and into the clearing. Leaving a large chunk of my hair behind in the bush.

'Oh, look at your arms. The friend pointed at my scratches.

'Yes, looks bad doesn't it. Thank you so much for helping me. I felt so silly, but I walked off the track to look at some mushrooms and then could not find it again. What a relief to be back on track again,' I explained.

Both the ladies smiled at me.

'Oh, dear you must be frightened. Will you be ok?' the first lady asked.

'Yes, I'll be ok, and thank you again for all your help,' I praised them both again. The ladies smiled back and turned to continue walking along the track.

That was enough walking in this bush for me today and I proceeded slowly along the track back to my car, which was parked at the visitors center. As I walked back, I reflected on my experience. Although it was not a pleasant one, strangely I felt like I wanted to learn more about bush survival. The bush definitely earned my respect today and I will make sure not go off the track ever again.

Melissa Gunn: Subtropical paradise

When The Lion Rocked (1960's)

Karen Morris-Denby

We danced the twist then made a wish
to the music of the sea
We did not know how our future would go
we left it a mystery
Elvis was groovy Cliff Richard a smoothie
we wondered what life would bring
We sat on the beach where no parent could reach
' Ten Guitars' we loved to sing
We ate cold pies under a star filled sky
then raced up the grassy hill
When the tide rolled in we made such a din
life at Piha was such a big thrill
The full moon would glimmer on wet sands like a mirror
our old Morrie Minors stood by
We rocked and we rolled never did as we were told
just waited for our togs to dry

When the seasons changed we never felt strange
       as we rode every wave to hang five
The Lion stood strong we would always belong
       our plan was to forever survive
As we drifted away when our hair went grey
       for some of us our dreams came true
Then we came back to tread the same track
       the Lion stood as remembered on cue
For the mates who had left we felt utterly bereft
       but we knew that we all must die
Our ashes will float when they are thrown from a boat
       some will stand with tears in their eyes
Piha Beach in its glory will never tell our story
       as the waves come in at high tide
How we lived the good life no worry or strife
       and how we all enjoyed a wild ride.

Susan Glamuzina: Lion Rock

Waitākere Calling

Rebecca Hare

Tracks tattoo the grooves and
 Mounds of her back, turned
Against a disconnected city.
West- facing, the kuia guards
Her coastline, her waterfalls
Cascade into infinity pools
Limbs stretching into warm
Tempestuous waters, she offers
Edges of herself, hugs her friend
Te Tai-o-Rēhua / The Tasman Sea.
Here for you.

Nikau stands gently sway
Nestled into the folds of her
Green quilted coat, breathing life
Into the sanctuary of her slopes.
Heritage seeds grow, tenderly
Regenerating her rainforest cloak
Lush, lowland bush clings
A kererū safeguards her brood
Spreads protective wings against
Relentlessly fierce winds.
Sheltering you.

We drive her curvy scenic
Roads, inhaling her charm
Stopped by a hitchhiker's arm.
We share our egg sandwiches
Before visiting the Kauri Cathedral
Sing harmonies to the hollow
In sacred space communion.
Petrichor rises in the fragile
Damp, through filtered sunlight.
The pūpū- rangi / kauri snails are thriving.
Grateful for you.

Descending over the last hill
Sparkling waters tease.
I plunge into an invigorating
Salty welcome, her fingertips
Tickle in the foam. Contentedly
Speechless on the way home
Tree ferns wave their goodbye
In the fading light. Sea spray
Hangs in the thick, misty air
Is that Tahurangi / fairy folk I hear?
Playing for us.

Kōauau / flutes are calling
Willing us to stay a little longer.
To replenish us.
She will replenish you too.

Bush and Sky

Barbara Peterson

Darkest Before Dawn

Angela Reading

With sleep still resting on heavy eyelids
Falling out of bed in zombie state
Exiting through the front door softly
Gliding through black darkness
A fresh breeze makes me shudder
I drive down to French Bay
All is silent beside the carbon ink sea

Soon dawn's theatre will reveal all
In its early morning costume
As the sun slowly rises behind earth's surface
It fills the sky with fire, yellow golds, orange and red
Such joy, a perception of magnificence
Reflections sing out to my soul
As they bounce around on clouds and sea

Every morning the jewellery of day arrives

My footsteps become imprinted in smooth wet sand

Alone I am witness to this miracle unveiling

A majestic moment as waves gently lap

Daylight begins again to dazzle and delight

I think of artists like McCahon walking here

Artists gone now who created messages in sand

Then transcribed them onto canvas

So their mark making lives on

Angela Reading: Golden reflections

KareKare Beach

Gillian Moon

Stream of Consciousness

I remember…

Friday nights, leaving our Onehunga home, packed into the family car, Mum, Dad and us four kids heading across Auckland city towards a weekend away to an untouched, wild paradise.

Stopping at a Glen Eden sports ground for a Friday night dinner of fish n chips, followed by a pink marshmallow chocolate fish and stashes of Sparkles and Lifesaver lollies – Dad's treat.

I remember…

how the air would suddenly change as we left the city behind, as if we had crossed a line and entered another realm into the magic of Waitākere. I would wind down my window to smell, feel and breathe the change.

I remember…

leaving the smooth sealed road that led to Piha and turning into the dusty, winding gravel route down the native bush lined hill to Karekare beach. Our second home for weeks on end during the long sultry summer school holidays.

I remember...

   our bach nestled into native bush, the rudimentary concrete basement with a wringer washer machine, shower and septic tank toilet. The outside upstairs steps led to the living areas of kitchen, armchair area, side bunkrooms and the ink-black darkness of night. No street lights. The haunting call of the ruru echoing across the valley of darkness.

I remember...

   walking along the grassy track adjacent to the gravel road to get to the beach, enveloped in clouds of dust when the cars passed by. Jandal clad feet, towelling sun hats, white sunscreen plastered across our faces, beach towels slung over shoulders. Carefree and happy.

I remember...

   wide open expansiveness of the beach, tumble weeds and red hot black sand that shimmered like glistening diamonds. Damming the creek with driftwood and rocks provided hours of play, as did rolling down the sand dunes covered in wet black sand.

I remember...

   the trek across the sand to the wild west coast ocean. Some days the black sand was too hot to walk on so we would follow the creek barefoot looking for tadpoles and minnows along the way. When the wind came up the black sand that sparkled like diamonds would whip relentlessly against tog-clad bodies, and reduce us to tears.

I remember...

   being tossed and tumbled by wild waves and strong currents, black sand forever tangled in my hair and embedded in my scalp. I would often prefer to retreat to the calmness of the lagoon and to sit in the shade of the carved cliff at the base of the 'Watchman Rock'.

I remember...

family walks around the southern rocks, hanging onto forgotten, rusted railway remnants to navigate the rocky precarious 'path' leading to Whatipū Beach. Clambering down the rocks to cross at a sandy inlet— Mum on one side, Dad on the other—we waited, one by one, for the word 'go', sprinting   across the sodden sand the moment a wave had retreated, seizing the moment before the next giant one rolled in. We would walk to the old tramway tunnel at Tunnel Point before heading back the way we came.

I remember...

the countless walks through the oasis of Pōhutukawa Glade that we called 'Happy Valley'. Prolific birdsong, picnics, shady trees, endless games of 'hide n seek'.

I remember...

the magic of Karekare waterfall—native bush and pristine fresh water—a stark contrast to the salt and sand of the sea. Crossing a small wooden bridge, we would 'trip trap, trip trap' like the three Billy Goats Gruff, with one of us hiding beneath as the troll laying in wait.

I remember...

neighbourhood gatherings, 'elevenses' Mum would call them, us kids would play Frisbee, swing-ball or swim and play in the dammed up freshwater creek that ran through our property. We would swim, catch tiny freshwater crayfish in clear plastic bait-catchers then let them go.

I remember... the sleek black eel lurking in the depths of the dam, nipping at my dangling toes.

I remember...

early morning mushrooming with Dad in the dewy paddocks of a neighbouring farm, steam rising from fresh 'cowpats'.

I remember...

late night walking to see the magical display of glow worm lights. Hushed voices and torches dimmed.

I remember...

the reluctance as we left our beloved beach, travelling back to the city and our 'other' life.

Karekare Beach, home of my heart I remember.

Karekare

Sue Gee

The Lookout

Marco Glamuzina

The sound of nature fills my ears on the *lookout at the top of the hill*

almost untouched by humans as I look to my west on a *lookout on the top of the hill*

To my east a vast city framed by Rangitoto on the *lookout at the top of the hill*

To my north is rolling hills covered in rain forest with towers erecting from the peaks on the *lookout at the top of the hill*

Water vibrant blue as I look south surrounded by small beaches and farmland on the *lookout at the top of the hill*

Sun beams down on me as I feel my skin start to burn on the *lookout at the top of the hill*

Stone kererū stands above me on the *lookout at the top of the hill*

I am at peace on the *lookout at the top of the hill*

Marco Glamuzina: Lookout

Thank You Sunshine

Yazhini Kandheswari

Trapped beneath bodies through lingering nights,

Thank you, sunshine, for each day that you rise.

Your brightness is all that can give me life.

My darkness appears only in your light.

Dwindling as you dim behind a misty cloud,

Agony dissolves me. Will you come back out?

I call for the wind, for as the breeze hardens

In the crispness of your rays, my silhouette sharpens.

As evening falls, voices are hushing.

My tall, thin frame is stretched into nothing.

Again till dawn, you will be deeply missed.

For without you, sunshine, I do not exist.

Drone

Edna Heled

A Waitākere Werewolf

Melissa Gunn

At the western end of the Manukau Harbour there is a sandbar. To the north of the harbour mouth lie series of wide, windswept, surf-pounded, black- sand beaches. Most have crumbling clay cliffs; some have sand dunes, swamps, or lakes. Each beach is backed by the expansive, forested, Waitākere Ranges. Although many people live in and around these forested hills, there is enough wilderness to hide a lot. Even, perhaps, a pack of werewolves.

"Oi, Seth. Get back here or they'll see you!" My command was an angry whisper, but there was no doubt that Seth heard it. He flattened his ears a little, dropped to a crouch, but didn't move.

"Seth! I'll tell Mum you're spying on two-footers again if you don't come now. I mean it!"

Predictably enough for a teen werewolf, my idiot brother glanced back at me, then crawled another foot forward through the bush, closer to the edge of the lake. Closer to the humans.

I crossed my arms in annoyance. I didn't really want to tattle on Seth to Mum, but if anyone saw him spying on the scantily clad humans swimming in the dune lake, they'd assume he was a stray dog, with his wild, unkempt fur that matched his hair in human form. That would mean the council would start setting baits, or worse, employ hunters with guns. The whole pack could be at risk thanks to Seth's fascination with two-footers. Or rather, with one specific two-footer.

"You know there's no point, right?" I leaned against a kānuka trunk, two- footed myself at the moment: unlike Seth, I had moved past the dangerous teen years and my frontal lobe was connected. I could weigh up risks. That's why I had an old dog-leash in one hand and a denim jacket slung over my shoulders, to keep off the sun and mosquitoes. A two-piece bikini I'd picked up on the sand late one night after the surfers had gone home covered the most important bits.

Unlike the impulsive Seth, I could stroll out onto the lake shore and pretend I'd just gone for a quick plunge in the lake, and that my brother was an errant dog that I absolutely had under control - 'see, officer, my leash broke'.

Cicadas shrilled with insistent late-summer madness. The sky was blue and cloudless above the bush, and the clay track had developed cracks wide enough to fall into as the drought bit deeper.

That was why we were at the lake, of course. Only a few of the streams in the Waitākere Ranges flowed year-round, and one of them fed into the blissful dune-backed fresh-water lake in front of us. The last week of the summer holidays was upon us, and the two-footers were running as wild as werewolves, revelling in the water as – let's face it – I longed to do too.

"Just change, Seth. She's not going to talk to you if she thinks you're a dog, and she's not going to talk to you if you're two-footed. At least if you change, we'll get a swim." I was impatient for that swim, sweaty from the walk here and itchy from mosquito bites. Even now I could imagine the soothing touch of the sun-warmed water, cooler as it got deeper. We could paddle around the floating reed-islands and pretend we had the place to ourselves.

Instead, Seth had spotted a girl who he'd instantly decided was the love of his life, and was now refusing to change. I wasn't sure if he was being shy or stupid. Probably both, knowing my brother. I decided I'd have to try a different tack.

"I'm going to slide down the dune into the lake. Bet you I'll get there first." Start a competition: always a good option when trying to motivate teen werewolves. Werewolves of any age, really. I debated leaving the leash and jacket behind, but then I'd have to come back to this spot. I'd rather get Seth moving, and return via the stream to our pack, once I'd had my swim. Perhaps I'd drop them on the sand just before I jumped into the water.

Trusting that my idiot brother would follow me (since my plan would take him closer to the girl who was still splashing around on the edge of the lake, squeaking about how cold it was), I strode off. I followed the human track around the water instead of leaping straight in the way I usually would. But I had to veer off it to reach the giant dune. The moment I stepped onto the sand I realised I'd forgotten a key part of my two-footer ensemble: jandals. The sand burnt with the fire of a thousand suns. I winced from one foot to another.

Could I still make it to the dune's crest? Perhaps I wasn't completely unlike my brother, because I broke into a run, heading uphill. Maybe I could reach the top of the dune without burning my feet, if only I was fast enough. I gritted my teeth against the pain and ran faster.

I was nearly at the top when shouts rang out. My hearing was still wolflike in my two-footed form, and I identified the lupine undertone of one of those shouts, even as I realised that unfamiliar pack scents were being blown my way. Behind me, Seth whimpered as he set foot on the sand. I hesitated, slipped, and lost my footing in the hot sand. Before I knew it, I was rolling back down the dune's face.

"Look out below!" someone yelled. It wasn't me.

A guy from the other pack whooped, and as I rolled, I noticed footsteps pounding after me. Far away at first, they approached at speed: someone was doing what I had planned to do, running down the dune towards the water.

Sand flew around me, working its way into my mouth, my nose, my ears. Shrieks sounded nearby, and I was aware of two-footers scrambling out of the way. That meant I had just moments before-

My body soared through a couple of feet of empty air before I hit the surface of the lake. I gasped with the shock of the water, choking on a mouthful of waterweed-flavoured water before I regained my senses enough to close my mouth. My feet hit the sandy, silty bottom, and I pushed off, stroking for the surface. As I was about to reach it, another body plunged in beside me.

I shrieked with surprise, then closed my mouth before I swallowed any more lakewater. I wasn't *that* thirsty. Blinking duckweed out of my eyes, the first thing I saw was Seth. He'd abandoned his lupine form and was swimming along the edge of the lake, butt-naked. That idiot! He was closing in on his quarry. I just hoped he'd have the sense to stay in the water; at least that way his nakedness was half-way acceptable.

But his wasn't the body that had plunged in next to me – he was too far away for that. I looked around. The leash draped over one of those reed-covered islands, one end dangling in the water.

As I watched, a duck tried to nibble on it before spitting it out in disgust. Good thing I hadn't hit the island instead of going into lake - that would have hurt. My jacket, however, was... in the hands of an unfamiliar werewolf.

He trod water next to me, his soaking wet t-shirt and boardshorts clinging to his nicely proportioned body. About my age, he also wore his two-footed form. However, his yellow eyes and wolfy scent left me in no doubt as to what he was.

"This yours?" He hefted the sodden jacket, which streamed water. A smile lurked around the corners of his mouth.

"What's it to you?" Not knowing what pack this attractive specimen was from meant I was on uncertain ground. Was he one of the power-hungry Centrals, our main rivals? Or from further afield?

His smile became genuine, white teeth and just-a-bit-longer-than-human canines gleaming in the sun. "If it was your brother's I'd heft it into the centre of the lake so he stops ogling my sister. But if it's yours... I'd heft it onto the reeds to dry so I could ogle you instead."

I opened my mouth to claim it, then did a double-take as his words rearranged themselves in my head.

"Um..."

"I'm Rick," he said, holding out his free hand to shake. "Woodside Pack."

The tension I'd been feeling dropped away – this was no Central werewolf. Woodside had a good reputation. I took Rick's hand and shook it briefly. "Miranda. Can I have my jacket back now?"

"Sure. But won't you join me in a swim? That sand was hot!" The hint of complaint in his voice made me smile.

Rick tossed my jacket onto the reeds where it would dry, and leant back into the water's embrace, gazing up at the blue sky as I had done earlier.

I let my feet float to the surface as I relaxed. I was free to be myself, and my brother hadn't made the worst choice ever. If I swam long enough, my jacket might even dry out before I had to put it on again. "Sure. You can tell me what brings you to the Ranges." I swished my arms gently through the lakewater, then turned over in the water, the spirit of competition rising in me. I felt surreptitiously for the edge of the floating reed island with a foot. Yes, it was close enough for a push-off. "But first, I bet I can beat you in a swimming race to the waterfall and back." I launched myself off the reed island, diving under for a smoother start to my self-declared race. When I surfaced, Rick was just behind me. I grinned, and swam harder, glorying in the heady rush of the race, and admiring the diamonds of sun-jewelled water that flung themselves into the hot blue summer sky.

Sue Gee: Company Stream - A dog with a stick crosses a tributary

Taitomo

Tonchi Glamuzina

Keyhole floods with light
Inviting exit
Wild waves seem calm

Wet feet slip
Rush! Rush! Rush!
Shirts and shorts soaked

Surf surges
Cavernous cave awash

Susan Glamuzina: Keyhole

Impact

Alexandra Fraser

you are always alone
when you enter the bush

whether you go
with a hearty crowd

packed and booted
keen to reach the trig

or a small excursion
from a parked car

following an enticing sign
 a solitary wander

with bottle of water
and mobile phone

each step the track takes you
further to the unknown

the solidity of trees
hundreds of years old centuries old

confronts you
with your fragile mortality

the birdsong does not
suppress the silence

and the thin rays of sunshine
are stripped of their warmth

Six is very young
to be lost in the bush

even with a seven year old
companion

as it gets darker and darker

our laughter becomes tight
the words of cheer shrill

the morepork alarms
the hedgehog confuses

the possums mock
supplejack trips

and we cannot see our way
so that the only path
is forward

Gannet Colony

Melissa Gunn

Revival

Suzanne Weld

Liv steers into the carpark, swerving sharply away from the ruts in the soggy gravel. She pops her seatbelt, slams the car door and slings her rucksack over her shoulders. A sooty black pīwakawaka squeaks, fidgets and flits at the edge of the bush. Liv sees a slight gap in the foliage and makes a beeline for it. She doesn't need council signage to find the beach.

Her path is cool underfoot, softened by leaf skeletons and spongy delicate humus. Heavy, droplets slide off the broadleaf canopy and plop around her. Vestiges of the storm that taunted her all the way from Titirangi to Huia remain.

The air is thick with vigour, mauri, and Liv knows this is just what she needs. She closes her eyes, inhales and exchanges misty breath with ngahere. It's been way too long since she navigated this trail and it feels as narrow as a tightrope. She's forced to slow her pace but she's still too agitated to sense the forest's heartbeat.

Sudden flapping and crashing in the canopy and Liv stops. She catches sight of a bouncing branch where just out of reach is a kererū, head cocked to the left, atop soft cream and turquoise plumage. Beady eyes interrogate her. Staccato notes of a tūi pierce the white noise of cicadas, disrupt the chatter in her head. Through the discord, she can just pick out Tangaroa's baritone rumble.

The forest is sparser now and Liv's skin prickles in the dry heat. Brittle twigs and dessicated gorse pods crackle and pop as they expire in the sun. She picks up speed, hurtles past a palisade of blackened manuka stems and through a tunnel of viridian flax. And there, between the dunes, is the abiding line where the sea caresses the sky to infinity.

The ground shifts underfoot and in her haste, Liv lurches forward, her foot snared in a snake of pingao rearing up from the sand. The broad, black beach glistens, as alive in the bright light as the waves which sparkle and beckon. Hearing Tangaroa's welcoming roar and the karanga of reeling gulls, Liv sprints across the scalding sand, strips off her rucksack, shorts and t-shirt, and throws them into the high tide's line of dried seaweed, broken shells and driftwood.

On the West Coast, the Tasman Sea is a force to be reckoned with as it beats the beach and retreats, beats and retreats. She hurdles the churning waves, then dives in and swims for her life. She's a strong swimmer and ploughs through the surf to a calm where she bobs, face upturned to the cloudless sky, until the shock of the icy water hits her. It's a sudden wake up call, a welcome distraction that clears her mind of dissonant chatter. Each and every cell of her body hums to the song of the surf. She tastes salt on her top lip, blinks grit from her eyes. The sky is deepening to dark indigo and all around her, foamy white crests shift ceaselessly against it; they reach and retract, reach and retract.

Liv looks landward across the beach. Black sand sparkles with tiny diamonds. Rocks and caves are darker than night and she wonders about their shadows and stars. Waitākere rises, its lush, green cloak a tapestry embroidered by time. Old man mānuka lean into the mountains, seeking refuge from the blast of the sea.

A rogue wave crashes over her and suddenly she's tumbling upside down, down and over, over and down. Twisting and churning, as flimsy as kelp, in moana's muted depths. Liv knows to relax and roll with the surging currents, to wait till she's pushed back up. Then, she's gulping and gasping, and when she's dragged under again, for a split second she fears that this is it, that she's about to be rolled into an early grave.

She kicks out and up.

Up, up towards the liminal space between sea and sky. There's dead calm, as if she's been snared somewhere between living and not living. Like that ethereal moment between dreaming and waking; when night becomes light.

She sees strange, silvery light on the horizon and, for a while, is mesmerised by distant waves kissing the sky.

Suddenly she's cold and shivering. Seeing streaky clouds racing in from the south, she sets off, strong strokes chopping through the restless surf. She drags herself from the tide and runs over sodden sand. Her heart is still racing at the high tideline, where she scrubs the salty surf from her skin, pulls on her t-shirt and wraps her damp towel around her waist. Throwing her rucksack over her shoulder, she races back, picking her way through the clawing pīngao to find the path between the dunes.

In the shelter of the forest, her pace and breath slow. Soothed by the soft, familiar track underfoot, she falls back into Waitākere's rhythm. High above, the forest ceiling is an intricate mosaic where leafy canopy hands reach for one another but don't quite touch. Now and then, between the tall crowns of kahikatea, kauri and rimu, dense shafts of sunlight stream like celestial affirmations. She feels the pulsing green light of the understorey, the caress of verdant undergrowth. She feels ngahere's heartbeat.

Liv reaches out and up for reassurance from ancient trees, the kaitiaki of Waitākere. She feels the wairua, the genius loci, the essence of this place. She recognises the incantations of cascading streams and the timeless symphsonia of birdsong. She feels ngahere breathing gently through her and knows that she too will sing.

Emerging from ngahere's fold into sunlight, Liv is enlivened but calm. Just as she reaches her car, the rising notes of riroriro signal more rain. She drives back to the city, the storm in her wake.

Angela Reading: Rays

At Piha

Ron Riddell

I still think it's Sunday
a day of rest and repose
wave- watching at Piha
I still think it's tapu
after treading black sand
and fording the stream
I still think it's sacred
this day walking at Piha
dawdling, waiting for sundown
the rose-gold shimmering
from the union of sea and sky
one ending, one beginning

A Moment Captured

Tonchi Glamuzina

Sounds a-beautiful

footsteps abound

cicadas chirp

dog barks

decaying leaves

tūī lands roughly

berries fall

blue sky and soft white cloud

Lost Keys

Ashley Lindsay

There's a hole in the sand with my keys at Piha. My four-year-old tells me they aren't lost. Just *buried*. "Don't worry, mama. You'll find them!" She shrieks with laughter. Her pink and blue seahorse rashie is layered with black sand. It's streaked over her face too, and stuck to her arms all the way up to her elbows. She's been digging holes. Deep ones.

"If you show me where the keys are," I say with a calm voice, "we can get an ice cream."

She flashes a mischievous smile. "They aren't lost. I marked the spot with a stick."

For a moment, relief washes through me. But then I take a closer look at the three-square meters of sand in front of me. Dozens of short pieces of driftwood are punched into the sand like birthday candles.

"Which stick are they under?" My voice is less calm. And I cast a wary eye to the sky where the sun is starting to dip.

Amelia puts her hands on her hips and says, "I'm not telling. You have to *dig* to find them."

"Can you give me a clue?"

She shuffles over to the stick closest to our beach towels. An auspicious, spindly, black one.

"Is it there?" I ask, crawling closer to her. She dramatically clamps her mouth shut.

I try the bribe again. "We can have ice cream."

"Vanilla?"

"Yes, vanilla."

She beams at me and hands me her red plastic shovel. "They're right here." She points to the black stick. I take the shovel and dig. After a few scoops, a glint of silver catches my eye. I excavate my set of keys and we evacuate the beach to the ice cream store. Amelia is bouncing at my elbow, demanding vanilla ice cream with sprinkles. I reach into my bag for my wallet. It's gone.

I look to Amelia who flashes me a mischievous smile. "It's not lost. Just *buried*."

Ashley Lindsay: Land ship

Running the Pipeline Track

Caroline Masters

The day begins
with my knees grumbling,
the first frost glowing
on the dark grass
beside the rolling track.

My watch buzzes
with an intrusive stream of stats—
enough data for a moon landing.

Through the pulse of crickets,
a ruru rings, sharp and strange,
like a cordless phone
dropped in the bush.

Far above, a conga line of lights
wobbles across the sky:
Starlink satellites,
winking out, one by one,
behind a cloud.

Each footfall draws me
into the moment,
beyond the orbit
of screen-lit hours.

There's Puanga,
bright above the black kānuka,
and Matariki
fading in the orange light.

Up the broad back of a hill,
body crackling with joy and struggle,
breath bursting white.

At the top,
I press my frozen fingers
to my mouth and breathe,
misty heat ascending
into the still, starry sky.

Latia, the Bioluminescent Limpet

Shaun Lee

Walking through the Waitākere Ranges at night, I worry about the world while documenting various tiny animals. The future often feels dark to me— human impacts on our wild places weigh heavily on my mind. Latia, the bioluminescent limpet, is one of the most fascinating creatures I've encountered in the Waitākere Ranges. My first experience with them was enchanting. Freshwater scientists had told me about these limpets, and I set out to find them, unprepared for their magic. When disturbed, Latia release a glowing slime as a defence mechanism—a luminescent display just a bit brighter than a glow-worm. Discovering them added wonder to my night outings. Latia limpets are rare, only found in the North Island of Aotearoa. They thrive in clear, stony streams where the freshwater remains close to pristine. Sadly, such places are becoming increasingly scarce in New Zealand. In the Waitākere Ranges, I know of only a few locations where they can still be found. My favourite spot once had an abundance of them—many per square metre. It was a place of wonder and beauty that I thought was safe from human impacts. That changed after the devastating floods of Auckland's Anniversary Weekend and Cyclone Gabrielle. The floods ravaged the stream, stones were tumbled clean of life.

The Latia limpets disappeared. For two years, I searched, finding nothing. The Latia seemed gone. Tonight, though, after a half-hour search, I found one— a single limpet, clinging tightly.

It's only one, but it feels like something more. A small light remains.

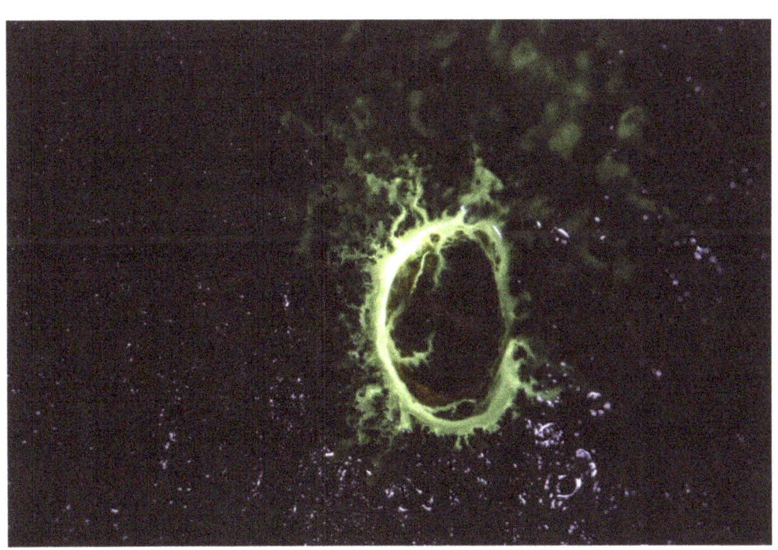

Shaun Lee: Latia, a bioluminescent limpet

Biographies

Akenese Faletigoai I am a 42 year old mama of two beautiful boys Labronz and Logan, and our wonderful dog Bella. We love going out on hikes at Waitakere Ranges, spotting hidden gems, of splendid scenery that spill out in spectacular ways only nature can design.

Alexandra Balm writes poems, short stories, and essays. Her work was published in Aotearoa New Zealand, Australia, America, and Europe (Czech Republic, Greece, Romania). In *More Deaths Than One* (2014), Garry Forrester called her "the mother of metamodernism." Alexandra's debut poetry collection, *Transformation*, was published in 2023 (Scripta Manent, Napier).

Alexandra Fraser has lived in the beautiful Tāmaki Makaurau most of her life She has been published in NZ and overseas for years and is working on her third collection. Previous collections are Conversation by Owl Light and Star Trails (both pub Steele Roberts).

Poet/teacher **Amanda Eason** has 4 collections published by NZ and UK poetry presses. Her work has appeared in numerous magazines and anthologies in both countries eg. NZ - Landfall, The Listener. UK - The Observer, New Statesman and Society. Amanda co-convenes *Titirangi Poets* monthly at Titirangi Library and gives Readings and Workshops.

Angela Campbell is a scribbler based in Auckland, New Zealand. For any success she has, she wishes to acknowledge Mrs Bull, her primary school teacher, and all dedicated educators whose passion makes a difference in the lives of children.

Angela Reading is a Titirangi Painter Poet Performer. She has been a student at Elam under the tuition of Fiona Pardington and Judy Millar. She has worked in the movie industry on "The Savage Islands", "Sylvia" and many more. Angela was part of "Marvellous Drama Group" that won several awards.

Anni Docking is a New Zealand poet, wordsmith and social entrepreneur. Graduating from University of Auckland with a B.A. (Hons) in English Literature and Education, she also holds a Diploma of Business Studies from Massey University. She finds artistic inspiration from nature and loves to explore forests and oceans. In addition to writing poetry and narrating her Irish heritage, Anni enjoys running marathons in remote corners of the planet. An established member of NZ Society of Authors, Anni's profile can be found here: https://authors.org.nz/author/annette-docking/

Ashley Lindsay is a YA and historical fiction author based in Auckland, New Zealand. She completed a Ph.D. in Chemistry, but writing has always been a passion of hers. Ashley likes to write strong, character- driven stories that take place in interesting and unusual settings. She has two co-written YA novels, *When the Rain Falls* and *The Price of Pandemonium* with Sarah Anderson under the pen name, Sasha A. Linderson. Website: https://www. lindersoncreations.com/

Barbs Peterson has previously had writing included in indie publications, such as "Ramble On: A celebration of walking in New Zealand" by Z.R. Southcombe and "Tales of the Domain Summer '22" curated by Auckland Writers. She regularly contributes at open mic storytelling evenings and can be followed on instagram at at https://www.instagram.com/barbsjp/ where she sometimes shares her writing and cat photos.

Bog Bakaric is a published author whose unique Croatian Crime series Blood Honour is currently with editors.

Bruce Wyness grew up in a country town close to beaches, rivers and farmland. After a career in the corporate world and time as a self-employed furniture maker Bruce rediscovered the joy of writing. He is an avid reader and observer of people and uses that to help craft his stories.

Carl Kjellberg worked for many years as a community support worker and has recently retired. As a child, he was encouraged to read and spent many hours frequenting local libraries and devouring many books, particularly science fiction. He is currently an active member of the Waitākere writer's group.

Caroline Carlyle A poet, writer, and artist. Caroline was raised in a literary-loving family. An active member of various writing groups such as I.W.W. NZ, she has claimed numerous awards such as Emerging Poet Award in the Kathleen Grattan Competition 2016, and runner-up in the 2023 Michele Whitecliffe Art Writing Prize.

Caroline Masters is a writer and teacher from Laingholm. Her work has appeared in various journals and anthologies. In 2023, Caroline was awarded the Kathleen Grattan Prize for her sequence of poems. She edits *Poetry Fridays*, an online journal for children's poetry, and has produced several anthologies of children's writing.

Cathryn Davy. This is my first attempt at writing poetry. Inspired by my good friend Sue and a snap shot from the beautiful Waitakere area.

Chris Reed is a high school English teacher from Auckland. He is an award-winning writer, musician and teacher with a beautiful wife and two wonderful daughters. Being a part of the Auckland Writers collections has been a real honour.

Deborah Leigh is a Titirangi native and former nurse, midwife and technical writer who enjoys writing poems and/or vignettes to create reflections, ponderings and/or mementos.

Denise O'Hagan holds a Master of Creative Writing from AUT. Her poetry has appeared in *Fresh Ink Anthology, NZ Poetry Society Anthology, Fast Fibres, The Blue Nib, Tarot, Live Encounters Aotearoa and Takahē magazine*. She enjoys writing poetry inspired by nature and her experiences and writes novels in contemporary fiction.

Di Nash is a doctor and finds in writing poetry a way of expressing herself that exists nowhere else. She lives in Titirangi on the ridge of South Titirangi Rd. She never tires of the bush and the sea views from there, and the beauty of the ranges.

Edna Heled is an artist, art therapist, counsellor and travel journalist living in Auckland. She studied Film & TV (BFA), Visual Arts (Diploma), Art Therapy (MA) and Psychology (BA Hons). Her writing includes short stories, poetry, travel writing and non-fiction. She is widely published in NZ, Australia, USA, UK and more. This is her fourth time participating in The Auckland Writers anthologies.

Élise Cater is a teen writer of surrealist fantasy who loves cats and herbs. She also enjoys visual art. She likes to twist words into poetry.

Fiona d'Young has always been a secret writer and is now slowly sharing her words with others. She lives in Titirangi and has been under the thrall of the Waitākere Ranges for the last fifteen years.

Frankie Glamuzina is a 13-year-old boy who has been published in all the 'Tales of…" Auckland anthologies and Upstart Magazine.

Growing up in Tāmaki Makaurau, **Gillian Moon** spent many weekends and school holidays at her family's bach at KareKare Beach during the 1970s and early '80s. She is a freelance writer and facilitator of *Journal Writing for Wellbeing* and *Memories to Memoir* workshops. Now based in Tairāwhiti, she is blessed with four daughters and four mokopuna . wired4wordsnz@gmail.com FB: Wired4Words

Ila Selwyn has published three poetry collections: *two sisters, 2011 dancing with dragons, 2018 slipping between, 2022*. She is hoping to get her next collection out his year.

Jenny Clay explores creativity visually and through words. The natural environment is very important to her, and she has spent much of her adult life in the Waitākeres among the tree ferns, rewarewa, and nikau.

Joel Ramos is a dual citizen of New Zealand and the Philippines. He loves the Waitākere Ranges, frequenting Piha, Titirangi and Cornwallis. He visits Arataki Visitor Centre each time he has a guest in Auckland. After stumbling upon Sue's haiku workshop, Joel wrote his first haiku for this anthology.

Juliet Yates, IWW member, concerned for our environment.

Justine Newnham works as a full-time gardener and studying horticulture part time. In her spare time, she likes to write. She wrote a short story and a couple poems for the last Anthology of Dominion Road. She was diagnosed with dyslexia late in life and wants to encourage other neurodiverse people to give writing a go too.

Karen Morris-Denby loves all forms of creative writing. Her passion is writing short film scripts but enjoys penning poetry, haiku haibun and flashfiction. Karen has had her writing published in print and online. The conclusion to her previous scripts in 'Dominion Road' and 'Hauraki Gulf' can be read on https://kazzel.wordpress.com

Kerry Clark has been story-telling all her life. After a career in teaching, she left work to focus on writing. Kerry has had articles and flash fiction published overseas and 3 picture books published in NZ as well as a ukulele book for children.

Kim Adams took a poetry workshop with Sue Glamuzina which she really enjoyed, where she wrote a poem for this anthology.

Laura Whitaker-Hill is a writer based in Tamaki Makaurau Auckland, who loves wrestling with words to create poetry, flash fiction and short stories. Her favourite spot in the Waitākere Ranges is the wild, windswept Whatipū Beach. She'd also love to see a kōkako one day.

Laurie Ross is a Lifetime Campaigner for Human Rights, Justice and Abolition of War. Co-ordinator of West Auckland Peace Group 1982 and Director of New Zealand Nuclear Free Peacemakers. Grandmother, musician, singer songwriter, dancer, rational mystic and poet of Huia and Titirangi. Cultural event coordinator for the Well Being Eco-Peace Economy Aotearoa.

Lee Simpson is a New Zealand author crafting *twisted romance*— stories where love collides with chaos. Think soulmates meeting at the wrong time, or passion entangled with danger (yes, sometimes even weapons). If you crave straightforward happily-ever-afters, her work might not be your cup of tea— but if you're drawn to raw explorations of love, loss, and deception, dive in. Instagram Lee_Simpson_author

Lincoln Jaques is a Tāmaki Makaurau based writer. His poetry, fiction, travel essays and book reviews have appeared in Aotearoa, the USA, Asia, the United Kingdom and Australia, including *Landfall, takahē, Live Encounters, Tough, Noir Nation, Burrow, Book of Matches, Anti-Heroin Chic, The Spinoff Friday Poem, Blackmail Press, Poetry Aotearoa Yearbook* and *Mayhem*. He was shortlisted for the 2023 inaugural I Te Kokoru At The Bay hybrid manuscript awards. He was guest editor for the 2023 and 2024 Live Encounters Aotearoa Poets & Writers editions.

Lucas Glamuzina is a 17-year-old recorded musician. He has written or created art for all the Auckland Anthologies to date.

Lucy Boermans is an interdisciplinary artist, researcher and design lecturer originating from Scotland. Boermans' research derives from a life-long love of language learning, and the sense-perception of movement, that is, the movement between everyday things, a kinesis that is embodied through us, and us through it, it being the moving world.

M Bulte is interested in history and changes in land use over time, and the way that people interact with the flora and fauna of their local area.

Marco Glamuzina has been published in the Domain and Dominion Road anthologies by Auckland Writers.

Marlene Milverton. Self-taught, and the recipient of several awards, she has had a passion for art since childhood and shared that enthusiasm tutoring watercolour classes for many years. After also working as illustrator for print and film I am now enjoying retirement and the pleasure of depicting nature in acrylics.

Matt Niederer is based in Rothesay Bay, Matt is a keen writer, currently studying creative writing at Massey and member of the North Shore Writers group.

Melissa Gunn is a multi-genre author who writes speculative and cozy fiction, as well as science & song books for kids. She is an enthusiastic scientist with a PhD in conservation genetics. She collects qualifications and hobbies, trying to change the way people see the world: through writing, science, art and more. Her books can be found at www.melissagunn.com

Dr Mels Barton is an environmental scientist turned coordinator, campaigner and environmental advocate, Mels works with community organisations. She is the Project Coordinator for Kauri Rescue, was a leading member of the Waitākere Rāhui campaign supporting Te Kawerau ā Maki and has been campaigning for better management and awareness of kauri dieback disease since it was discovered in Piha in 2006.. In the UK she worked for Environment Agency Wales for 9 years. She has lived in Titirangi since emigrating in 1999 & enjoys hanging out with her horses and dog.

Mt Albert Rangers Ashley Lindsay and Sue Glamuzina had a poetry, short story and art session at Mt Albert Rangers where they received some of the amazing work by their students and leaders. Scarlet Q, Rosie Shutterworth, Tilly Shutterworth, Zoey Bayliss, Savini Herath, Jessica Barr, Sophie Sewell, Keira Bailie, Amelia Barr, Elsie Beachman, Maryam Knowles, Alexia Brown

Philip Khouri has been making the passage through the Waitākere Ranges to the surf at Piha since the 1960's. The magic way station on the Piha Road is the Anawhata Road intersection. This is the point where the road tilts for the first time towards the coast and where on the way back to Auckland in the dark you pass through a portal between two worlds.

Piers Davies is a long-time poet and has been widely published in journals and anthologies in Aotearoa/New Zealand and overseas. He is co-facilitator of Titirangi Poets and co-editor of its Ezines and anthologies. He has also written feature films 'Homesdale', 'The Cars That Ate Paris' and 'Skin Deep'.

Raewyn Booth has lived in Titirangi with her husband for 34 years and loves being surrounded by nature. She has been putting pen to paper for many years and has only recently decided to share it with others. she finds writing and watching words come to life a joy.

Born in Tauranga, **Rebecca Hare** now lives and works in Auckland/Tāmaki Makaurau. A former primary school teacher, Rebecca has worked in media literacy, educational resource writing and publishing, and professional learning and development. Our nation's history, whānau, people, whenua and ocean swimming make her heart sing.

Ron Riddell is a writer with a deep commitment to ecology, on all possible levels: natural, social-temporal, philosophic and spiritual. He believes and works in the spirit of the transformative power of poetry and all creative human expression. At present, he divides his time between New Zealand and Colombia.

Rosie Lee writes forced proximity disaster romance set in Aotearoa (with a side serving of bad puns). Nothing tests humans quite like a little life- threatening bonding, but it's not always the girl who needs rescuing. If you like Storm in a Teacup you'll love her debut novel Surviving the Storm, just released. Follow her @rosieleeauthor on Instagram. www. rosielee.co.nz

Sarah Valentine is a mother, science teacher and writer. When those mythological moments of free-time find her, she loves to be outdoors with her whānau. You can follow her journey on instagram @writing_for_the_ joy_of_it

Shaun Lee is a designer, illustrator, and photographer advocating for the Hauraki Gulf and a citizen scientist studying kekeno mortality.

Sue Carpenter is a Junior Fiction and Young Adult author. She isn't ready to grow up so she keeps her mind young by writing for children. Sue doesn't want barriers between her readers and her imaginary worlds, so her books are written in simple language, are straight to the point and shorter – so easy to bite into and are dyslexic friendly. Follow Susieleenz on TikTok and Instagram, and see her books at www.susielee.co.nz

Sue Gee lives in Karekare, Te Wao Nui–a Tiriwa. She formerly photographed weddings and families. Now, as oral historian, she records peoples' accounts of their lives. Her work in both mediums is archived at Auckland Libraries. She is a member of Point Chevalier Pirates, a poetry group.

Sue Glamuzina loves having her feet in the sand and thoughts in the clouds. Her poetry has been widely published both nationally and internationally and she has led all of the Auckland writer anthologies.

Suzanne Weld was born and raised in Ōtautahi Christchurch but now lives in Tāmaki Makaurau Auckland. She works full-time and volunteers on the Auckland Committee of NZ Society of Authors. In her free time she is an avid gardener, nature lover, human rights campaigner and traveller, Recently, she has had short pieces of fiction, creative non-fiction and poetry published in four anthologies, and is preparing to publish her first novel.

Tania Leigh Pauling is a West Auckland artist and illustrator, works primarily with pastel and acrylic paint. She enjoys portraiture, photorealism, and children's book illustration. Tania's most notable work to date are the paintings for the book 'Magic Jack'. Tania is currently writing and illustrating a book inspired by her love for wildlife.

Tonchi Glamuzina is a newbie to writing after a family challenge to write poems for this anthology. He drew on what he had picked up from hours of listening to his wife's writing zooms.

Wolfgang B Sperlich trained as a linguist (with a PhD from Auckland University) and secondary teacher. His work in Oceanic languages includes the Niue Language Dictionary. His main academic work is a biography of Noam Chomsky. Wolfgang's poetry and prose has appeared in a number of publications. He lives in Huia.

Yazhini Kandheswari is a singer/songwriter who enjoys all things creative. Her poetry plays with personification and raw emotion, transforming pain into art. What started as an escape became a passion, and now, she writes to move and inspire others.

Susan Glamuzina: West coast beach

Read all the 'Tales of Auckland' Anthologies:

https://www.amazon.com/dp/B0DKLFGH5K

Tales of the Domain

Tales from Dominion Road

Tales of the Hauraki Gulf

Acknowledgements

Thank you to the many people who contributed their time and creativity to make this anthology possible.

We'd like to thank the Auckland Writers Anthology Committee for their countless hours of hard work, compiling, editing, and proofreading this manuscript—in no particular order, thank you to Melissa Gunn, Sue Glamuzina, Angela Campbell, Anni Docking, Ashley Lindsay and Suzanne Weld. Melissa Gunn also designed the cover design and arranged the interior formatting.

To Jade Du Preez, thank you for the anthology logo design and for IT support; to Ashley Lindsay and the Mt Albert Rangers, thank you for your continued contribution to this anthology.

To Kick Arts Radio, thank you for helping to spread the word of our project. Thank you to Titirangi Poets for hosting Sue for a day to focus on the anthology, and to RWNZ, IWW, NZSA and Poetry Live for letting your members know about the opportunity to submit work to this anthology, giving the anthology greater breadth and scope.

Finally, thanks to all the writers and artists who submitted poems, short fiction, non-fiction and art to this anthology—we couldn't do it without you. Your diverse and unique submissions demonstrate your love for the arts and for the Waitākere Ranges.

www.ingramcontent.com/pod-product-compliance
Lightning Source LLC
Chambersburg PA
CBHW061119100726
47911CB00013B/610